1/96 LAST

5/
/98

10/11 13x

AUG   1997

R

D0455461

Dreams
and Wishes

By the Same Author

The Dark Is Rising *sequence:*

Over Sea, Under Stone
(An Aladdin Paperback)

The Dark Is Rising
The 1974 Newbery Award Honor Book

Greenwitch

The Grey King
The Winner of the 1976 Newbery Award

Silver on the Tree
(Margaret K. McElderry Books)

Dawn of Fear
(An Aladdin paperback)

Seaward

The Silver Cow
illustrated by Warwick Hutton

The Selkie Girl
illustrated by Warwick Hutton

Tam Lin
illustrated by Warwick Hutton

Matthew's Dragon
illustrated by Jos. A. Smith

Danny and the Kings
illustrated by Jos. A. Smith

The Boggart
(Margaret K. McElderry Books)

Dreams and Wishes

Essays
on
Writing
for
Children

Susan Cooper

MARGARET K. MCELDERRY BOOKS

Margaret K. McElderry Books
An imprint of Simon & Schuster Children's Publishing Division
1230 Avenue of the Americas
New York, New York 10020

Book design by Becky Terhune
The text of this book is set in Fairfield.
Printed in the United States of America
First Edition

10 9 8 7 6 5 4 3 2 1

Library of Congress Cataloging-in-Publication Data
Cooper, Susan.
Dreams and wishes: essays on writing for children / Susan Cooper.
p. cm.
A collection of fourteen essays by and one interview with Susan Cooper, award-
winning author of numerous books for children, including The Dark Is Rising series,
on the subject of writing for children.
1. Children's literature—Authorship. I. Title.
PN147.5.C66   1996
808.06'8—dc20
95–31077
CIP
ISBN 0–689–80736–8

Page 198 constitutes an extension of the copyright page and contains the permissions
and acknowledgments for this book.

FOR JESS
IN LOVING MEMORY

Contents

"All [these] things are ready to be adapted to the world of a child, and they can be adapted simply by an intellectual effort; but anyone who enters the child's world, whose dreams and wishes in some way become merged into a child's dreams and wishes, will produce a better book than the writer who writes, as it were, from the top of his head. One will write a story about a rabbit who runs away and gets into mischief; the other will write *Peter Rabbit.*"

Margery Fisher, *Intent Upon Reading*

In the Beginning

I lost my professional innocence when I was thirty-nine. After my busy twenties, when I was a journalist in Britain, I had moved to America and become mildly reclusive, writing a newspaper column and assorted books, some of them for "young adults," while raising my two children, who were by now seven and eight. Married to a professor at MIT, I lived among scientists and engineers, and the world in which I wrote my books was entirely private. I never even read my reviews, feeling obscurely that neither praise nor blame were very good for the ego.

One escapist winter day, I was sitting on the porch of our little holiday house on one of the remoter British Virgin Islands, working on a book called *The Grey King*. A dinghy came chugging toward me over the blue water from the small hotel-island next door, which unlike ours boasted a telephone, and a voice shouted, "Susan! Phone call!" I ran for my boat, expecting an emergency, but found instead the warm voice of Barbara Rollock of the American Library Association, calling me from their midwinter convention with the news that my earlier book *The Dark Is Rising* was this year's Newbery Honor Book.

"Newbery Honor Book?" I said.

"The runner-up. The only one! For the Newbery Medal."

Tucked in my private world, I'd never heard of the Newbery

1

Medal. "Oh," I said rather ungraciously. "Er—thank you very much."

I went home in my boat. "Nothing wrong. Just someone telling me *The Dark Is Rising* missed winning a prize. I don't know why they bothered."

I was about to find out. Before long there were more phone calls, the first of them from my editor, Margaret K. McElderry. Normally a most reasonable person, she sounded faintly delirious. "Isn't it wonderful? You'll have to come to New York in July for the presentation. And Atheneum will give a dinner in your honor!"

"But I'll be back here in July. The children—"

"Susan, you *have* to come."

"But I didn't even win this medal!"

"Susan," Margaret said patiently, "you don't understand."

I didn't. But I began to learn, some months later, at the ALA Midsummer Convention during which the Newbery and Caldecott Medals (for the year's "most distinguished contribution to American literature for children") are actually presented. I discovered that there was a world out there filled with people who cared passionately about children's books; librarians and teachers and others who not only took such books seriously but even referred to, discussed and revered them as "children's literature." I was amazed and delighted—and also filled with horrified sympathy, when I found that the current winner of the Newbery Medal, Paula Fox, was going to have to make her acceptance speech before an audience of two thousand people. Margaret and I walked to our table through the babel of voices in the huge banqueting hall, and I said faintly in her ear, "I *never* want to win the Newbery Medal."

Two years later I won it, for *The Grey King*—and I too had to learn to talk. This book is the indirect result of that fact. As every winner of the Newbery or Caldecott Medal soon discovers, the small world of children's literature is full of conferences and festivals, workshops and institutes at which authors and illustrators are invited to speak, and the speakers' invitation list instantly opens to embrace anyone awarded a major prize. The prize-winning itself—provided you've written or illustrated a good book—is largely a matter of luck, depending on the quality and quantity of the other good books published that year, the personal taste of the judges, and the persuasive powers of any judge particularly excited by your own work. If you are lucky, you inherit not just that helpful little gold sticker on the jacket of your book but, in all the years to come, the repeated chance to work out lectures which examine the nature of your craft, your audience, and that other piece of good fortune that gave you your imagination.

My greatest good fortune as a writer brought me not a medal but my editor, Margaret K. McElderry, whose friendship and advice have illuminated my life for thirty years. This is the fifteenth book we have worked on together. In choosing the pieces for it, we found that no less than six of them owed their existence to the organizers of Children's Literature New England, Barbara Harrison and Gregory Maguire. For years these two ran the Center for the Study of Children's Literature (founded by Barbara in 1975) at Simmons College in Boston, until an explosive disagreement over administration blew them and most of their faculty—including Betty Levin, Jill Paton Walsh, John Rowe Townsend and Paul and Ethel Heins—into independence. The international one-week institute which this amazingly gifted group now holds each summer, as Children's Literature New England, has become a legend of imaginative scholarship. It's also one of my favorite weeks of the year. Only through CLNE do you find yourself at Oxford or Cambridge, Harvard or Trinity College Dublin, pondering the complexities of time or myth over a beer with Katherine Paterson or Ursula Le Guin, and a bunch of bright teachers and librarians who know far more about your readers than you ever will yourself.

My own children flicker in and out of this book, as if it were a photograph album charting their growing-up. Dear Kate, dear

3

Jon, thank you for the day when you insisted on being allowed to travel alone, aged nine and ten, from Boston to the ALA Convention in Chicago to see your mother awarded the Newbery Medal—and to spend hours gleefully going up and down in the Ritz-Carlton elevator with young Lee Dillon, son of the Caldecott winners Leo and Diane. My thanks too to Hume Cronyn, for many things, but particularly for helping me to cope with the terrors of public speaking ("SLOW," he used to write in the margins of my first lectures. *"GO SLOW!"*), to my friend and ex-husband, Nicholas Grant, and to Pamela McCuen for her patient work on manuscripts.

This book is dedicated to Jessica Tandy, actress and reader, who believed that children's books are also for grown-ups. She loved being given authors she hadn't yet discovered, and I loved giving her them: Lucy Boston, Penelope Lively, Philippa Pearce, Patricia Wrightson, Betty Levin, Nina Bawden, and on, and on. I didn't have to give her *The Dark Is Rising*. Twenty years ago in the Caribbean, at the time I mentioned earlier in this piece, there happened to be a couple of actors staying on the hotel-island that had the telephone. My husband and I were introduced to Hume Cronyn on a day when his wife was in bed nursing a sunburn.

Hume went back to their room. "I met a nice American called Nick Grant," he said. "We're going fishing. And his wife is a countrywoman of yours, Susan something. She writes children's books."

"Not Susan Cooper?" Jessica said.

"That's it," said Hume.

Jessica said, "She wrote that book I've been trying to get you to read for the last six months."

We could use a few more grown-ups like that.

SEEING AROUND CORNERS

A talk accepting the Newbery Medal for The Grey King, *given at the American Library Association Convention in Chicago, August 1976*

This year marks the centennial of the American Library Association and the bicentennial of the United States of America. It says a great deal for the rugged independence of the Children's Services Division that they should choose such an anniversary to award the Newbery Medal to a Limey.

A very nervous Limey, too. Not for that reason: I do, after all, live near Boston, where the history of the wicked British pursues me at every turn. Especially as recounted by my American children. No. My problem is one aspect of the Newbery familiar to those of you who have attended this ceremony before—the fact that the winner, accustomed to solitude as a hermit to his cell, can traditionally be expected to stand up here, before two thousand faces, absolutely rigid with fear.

I did think I'd found a way to overcome this problem. I happen to be very, very short-sighted. I should need only to remove my glasses, I thought, to be unable to see any one of these unnerving faces. I might even see something quite different. As one of my fellow-sufferers, James Thurber, once said, "Those of us who are half blind are luckier than you think. Where the rest of you see a paper bag blowing down the street, we see an old lady turning somersaults."

5

I gave up the idea about the glasses when I realized that if I couldn't see my audience, equally I shouldn't be able to see my speech. But Thurber's remark stuck in my head. He might just as well have been talking about another kind of minority group than the myopic: those of us who write books—like *The Grey King*—which are classified as fantasy. We live in the same world as the rest of you. Its realities are the same. But we perceive them differently.

We see around corners. It's a little like abstract painting, or poetry—and not at all like the realistic novel. The material of fantasy is myth, legend, folktale; the mystery of dream, and the greater mystery of Time. With all that haunting our minds, it isn't surprising that we write stories about an ordinary world in which extra-ordinary things happen.

Nor is it surprising that we should be read, today, mainly by children. Most of us, mind you, have no idea whether we are writing books for children or for adults. We write the book that wants to be written, and let our publishers tell us what it is. (And there I am luckier than most, since Margaret McElderry is the wisest and most sensitive editor-publisher I have ever known, anywhere.) But even though more adults are reading fantasy these days—in a flight, perhaps, from the realities of the machine back to the older realities of myth—even so, children are the natural audience for fantasy. They aren't a different species. They're us, a little while ago. It's just that they are still able to accept mystery. They don't bat an eye when you present them, within the framework of the world they know, with things like a flying horse, candles which burn bitter cold, a house in which yesterday will take place tomorrow. Nothing shakes them. Experience hasn't yet interrupted their long discovery. They still know the essence of wonder, which is to live without ever being quite sure what to expect. And therefore, quite often, to encounter delight.

Those of us who work in the arts never know quite what to expect either. Once upon a time, when I was about twenty-five years old, writing features for the Sunday *Times* in London, the

Literary Editor of the paper came into my office one day and dropped a press release on my desk. He said, "Read that. You ought to try it."

It was a notice from an English publishing house called Ernest Benn Limited. They'd been the original publishers of E. Nesbit, and in her honor they were offering a prize for what they called "a family adventure story." There was a deadline, and being a journalist I liked deadlines. (Needed them. I still do.) And it sounded like fun—so I did try. I invented three children called Simon, Jane and Barney, and a rather vague plot about villainy and hidden treasure. And I wrote a first chapter in which they traveled down from London to Cornwall by train for a summer holiday, as my brother and I had done as children.

And then a funny thing began to happen. The story, somehow, took over. My children were met at their destination by a very strange great-uncle named Merriman (why did I call him Merriman? I didn't know) and before I quite knew what I was doing, the plot began to change completely. I forgot all about the E. Nesbit prize and the family adventure story—and the deadline. And I found I was writing a fantasy, full of images which had haunted me since childhood but which I'd never thought to put into fiction. In the final version I even cut that first deliberate chapter. And there I was with a book called *Over Sea, Under Stone*. Which turned out to be the first movement in a symphonic pattern of five books—one of which is the reason I'm here today.

The pattern didn't emerge for a long time. I had no intention then of writing a sequel to *Over Sea*—though I did leave it open-ended, since I'd grown fond of the characters, especially the Merlin-figure called Merriman, and I didn't want to cut myself off from them forever.

About five years went by, in the space of which I married, came to America to live, wrote a couple of adult books, and had a baby. Then one snowy day I was cross-country skiing with my husband in Massachusetts, where we live. Now skiing is not a sport which produces great conversation. You just get the odd word, like

"Help!" So I was tramping along in silence, looking at the snow-drifts, seeing small trees sticking up out of the snow and thinking they looked like the antlers of deer—and then for no good reason at all, I suddenly knew that I was going to write a book, set for the most part in thick snow like this, about a small boy who woke up one birthday morning and found he was able to work magic.

I wrote the idea down, and forgot about it. I wrote two more adult books and had another baby, and three more years went by.

Then one day, something sent me back to reread the first children's book, *Over Sea, Under Stone*. Perhaps it was all my endless reading about Britain, prehistory, Britain, myth, folktale, Britain. . . . This went on all the time, because I'd never really mastered my homesickness, and I suppose I never shall. I reread something I'd had the old man Merriman say, about the constant recurrence in the history of Britain of the battle between the Dark and the Light. He'd said,

> The struggle between good and evil . . . goes on all around us all the time, like two armies fighting. And sometimes one of them seems to be winning and sometimes the other, but neither has ever triumphed altogether. Nor ever will . . . for there is something of each in every man . . .

And out of the shadows came again the image of the snow and the antlered snowdrifts, and the boy waking to find himself with powers he hadn't had before. And I started thinking, and scribbling, and I found coming into my head the pattern not only of that book but of the overall sequence of five, each dealing with different aspects of the long struggle. One was already written, four more were to come. So I made an outline of each, characters and plot and setting, and before I started to write the second, *The Dark Is Rising*, I wrote the last page of the very last book. That's still sitting in my file, and I shall use it—unchanged—when I find myself reluctantly reaching the place where it belongs later this year.

I would not have predicted all of that.

But of course, the whole process is a mystery, in all the arts. Creativity, in literature, painting, music. Or in performance: those rare lovely moments in a theater when an actor has the whole audience in his hand suddenly, like *that*. You may have all the technique in the world, but you can't strike that spark without some mysterious extra blessing—and none of us knows what that blessing really is. Not even the writers, who talk the most, can explain it at all.

Who knows where the ideas come from? Who knows what happens in that shadowy part of the mind, something between Plato's cave and Maeterlinck's Hall of Night, where the creative imagination hides? Who knows even where the words come from, the right rhythm and meaning and music all at once? Those of us who make books out of the words and ideas have less of an answer than anyone. All we know is that marvelous feeling that comes, sometimes, like a break of sunshine in a cloud-grey sky, when through all the research and concentration and slog— suddenly you are writing, fluently and fast, with every sense at high pitch and yet in a state almost like trance. Suddenly, for a time, the door is open, the magic is working; a channel exists between the page and that shadowy cave in the mind.

But none of us will ever know why, or how.

Just one thing can, perhaps, be charted, and that's the *kind* of stories that are told. If only looking back over your own work after you've done it, you can find some thread that runs through, binding it all together. The underlying theme of my *Dark Is Rising* sequence, and particularly of its fourth volume, *The Grey King*, is, I suppose, the ancient problem of the duality of human nature. The endless coexistence of kindness and cruelty, love and hate, forgiveness and revenge—as inescapable as the cycle of life and death, day and night, the Light and the Dark.

And to some extent, I can see its roots. My generation, especially in Britain and Europe, was given a strong image of good and bad at an impressionable age. We were the children of World

War II. Our insecurities may not have differed in kind from those of the modern child, but they were more concrete. That *something* that might be lurking in the shadow behind the bedroom door at night wasn't, for us, a terrible formless bogeyman; it was specific—a Nazi paratrooper, with a bayonet. And the nightmares that broke into our six-year-old sleep weren't always vague and forgettable; quite often they were not only precise, but real. We knew that there would indeed be the up-and-down wail of the air-raid siren, to send us scurrying through a night crisscrossed with searchlights, down into the shelter, that little corrugated iron room buried in the back lawn, and barricaded with sandbags and turf. And then there would be the drone of the bombers, the thudding of anti-aircraft fire from the guns at the end of the road, and the crash of bombs coming closer, closer all the time.

We took it all for granted, of course, like the gas masks we carried to school each day, the bits of shrapnel we collected after every air raid, the sight of Father's rifle and steel helmet in the polite English umbrella stand. And many families, like my own, were lucky; we were never physically hurt, we simply had a rather noisy war. But I don't think the sensation of threat, of an incomprehensible looming menace, ever went away.

The experience of war, like certain other accidents of circumstance, can teach a child more than he or she realizes about the dreadful ubiquity of man's inhumanity to man. And if the child grows up to be a writer, in a world which seems to learn remarkably little from its history, then the writing will be haunted.

Haunted, and trying to communicate the haunting. Whether explicitly, or through the buried metaphor of fantasy, it will be trying always to say to the reader: Look, this is the way things are. The conflict that's in this story is everywhere in life, even in your own nature. It's frightening, but try not to be afraid. Ever. Look, learn, remember; this is the kind of thing you'll have to deal with yourself, one day, out there.

Perhaps a book can help with the long, hard matter of growing up, just a little. Maybe, sometimes.

Thank you for giving me the Newbery Medal. The encouragement it brings is impossible to describe. But don't forget, Newbery winners come and go. Midsummer monarchs, that's what we are: set up, and honored, and then, by a natural rhythm, replaced. The real continuity, in this matter of keeping a channel between the imagination of the writer and the development of the child, is made year in and year out by you—librarians, teachers, storytellers, publishers. You remember—every one of us here does—that wonderful feeling of going into a library when you're young and have much yet to read. It's like entering Aladdin's cave: all those books, all that delight, waiting. And someone there to say, "Hey—try this one. It's good."

That's the channel of communication that *you* keep open, and without it we the writers would be powerless. The centennial of the American Library Association makes a happy moment to celebrate the fact. So—happy birthday, ladies and gentlemen. Please keep up the good work for at least another hundred years.

Talent Has Two Faces

A talk for the 6th Annual Festival of Excellence in Children's Books,
Fresno, California, April 29–30, 1977

Children's writers are, on the whole, a fairly modest bunch. We've learned to be, over years spent observing, with some amusement, our place in society. We've all met that friendly businessman at a party or in an airplane, the one who says jovially, "So you're a writer! I always wanted to meet a writer! What kinda books you write?" So we say, "Children's books," and his interest visibly wanes. "Oh," he says, "that's . . . cute. Do you draw your own pictures?" And we know we aren't *real* writers in his eyes, not like Harold Robbins or Jacqueline Susann.

Thus we are saved from conceit—and are inclined to tremble at challenges like the one presented by this conference, which is to define excellence in children's literature. It seems so arrogant to assume that one can define what excellence is in any field, let alone one with so few pretensions.

An English writer does have a slight advantage in this matter. There's no point in my worrying about appearing to be arrogant, because I already sound arrogant. You only have to listen for a moment to this English voice, relatively free of regional accent, all flinty consonants and rounded vowels. Mine isn't as pronounced as some, but you can hear the arrogance there. It's

12

saying to you, "This is my language, peasants. You've borrowed it. *I* come from the place where it was born."

I remember when I first came to the United States, I went into a drugstore in Washington, D.C., and I said to the girl behind the counter, "Please may I have some toothpaste?"

The girl stared at me. She said, "Say that again."

So I said it again. The girl looked away then, and yelled to an assistant on the other side of the store, "George! Come over here!"

I was beginning to be alarmed. I thought: have I said something wrong? Maybe Americans don't use toothpaste. Maybe toothpaste is some terrible word that means something quite different over here. Just as an Englishman in America, if he wants to wake a lady early in the morning, has to be careful not to say, as he would at home, "I'll come and knock you up at eight-fifteen."

George came across the store, and they both stood looking at me, and the girl said, "Say what you said, again, honey."

So I said nervously, "I just asked if I could have some . . . tooth-paste?"

And the girl gave George a big smile, and she said, "Don't you just *love* that British accent?"

But of course we don't have an accent. You do. It's our language.

I'm kidding, mostly. But where the English language is concerned I think perhaps the British really do have some small cause for arrogance. We are at present, in Britain, busily demolishing all the best parts of our educational system, but even so the products of that system still manage to handle their language rather more deftly than the average American high-school graduate does. Our teaching of English seems to be more successful. I don't know why. Maybe it begins earlier, or is more intensive. Maybe we make our children learn more. I do literally mean that—learning by heart great chunks of plays, or of verse, from the classics, without falling into the traps set by the dangerous word *relevance*. It's a marvelous way of getting a sense of the rhythm of our—yours and mine—rather beautiful language.

Or maybe it's just a matter of assumptions. I think it was W. H. Auden who pointed out that most literate people in Britain were still—in his day, at any rate—raised to think of the ability to express oneself in good prose as being an aspect of good manners. It's *polite* to use English well. It's certainly kind. And it's an antidote to an age in whose uncivil tongue, as Edwin Newman has pointed out, a president can describe a certain course of action as taking the hang-out road, the mayor of Boston can speak of young juveniles, psychologists speak not of children playing, but of children in a play situation, and a television newsman describe three families that had suffered kidnapping as having the same thing in common.

Don't misunderstand me: I'm not implying that British writers —or mayors, or television newsmen—are any better than Americans. What matters in the end is not the language, but the literature; not the bricks, but the house that is built out of them. I am suggesting, gently, that the writer who learns how to use the English language in England may start off his career with a better idea of how to use his bricks. He is more likely to be confident that he can handle the language well.

But here I'm risking arrogance again. Who is to say who can write well? What is good writing? Who's to judge?

There are no absolute standards. There are the rules of grammar, but that's all. You can't *prove* what you mean when you take two pieces of writing and say, "This one is good, and this one is bad." Scientific method can't be applied to the arts, even though numbers of wrong-headed people in schools and universities have been trying to do just that for years. You can show a child what happens when you divide fifteen by three, or how vinegar is an acid because it turns blue litmus pink, but you can't prove to him, in that same rational way, why a poem is written well. That's subjective. It's a matter of taste.

And you can't teach taste. You can only instill it, gradually, by a kind of osmosis, and encourage children to trust their own reactions. It's all a little like the list of sensations that the poet

14

Robert Graves set out once, as markers that tell you when you have written or read a true poem. "The hairs stand on end," he said, "the eyes water, the throat is constricted, the skin crawls, and a shiver runs down the spine." That could hardly be called a scientific and measurable criterion of judgment, but it's true; it works. Just one verse can do it:

> Fear no more the heat o' th' Sun,
> Nor the furious Winter's rages,
> Thou thy worldly task hast done,
> Home art gone, and ta'en thy wages.
> Golden lads and girls all must
> As chimney-sweepers, come to dust . . .

. . . and the hair does come up on the back of your neck, and you know that's the real thing. The child who is developing taste knows too, in the same instinctive indefinable way. You can tell, when you read him a poem or a story, and at the end of it he says, "Wow!"

This is a slippery business, the matter of judging books and words and stories. American schools and universities are full of courses in what is called Creative Writing. Yet I am convinced that you cannot teach creative writing. You can teach the structure of the language, the business of writing grammatical prose which is clear and easy to understand, and you can make sure that people read a very great deal between the ages of eight and eighteen. This is a basic apprenticeship for general literacy, and it should be forced upon anyone with an apparent gift for creative writing (though forcing is hardly necessary, because the owner of the gift is likely to seek it for himself, or herself). But the creativity itself cannot be taught.

The creative imagination is just there, in all writers, all artists. It's there from birth, like blue eyes or red hair, or the second set of teeth that's going to grow when the first teeth fall out. You can't teach it. You can uncover it in someone inhibited, and you can encourage it in someone without confidence, but those are things to do with character, which is quite another matter. In the long run, character is more important than talent. But the talent has to be there first.

As every teacher knows, the range of abilities and personalities in any one class of children is as uncontrollable as the weather. There is the fluent reader and the stumbler, just as there is the natural athlete and the klutz who drops every ball; the child with a gift for mathematical concepts and his bewildered neighbor who is barely numerate. In many fields, excellence is largely a matter of luck. You can't be a great musician if you're born with a tin ear. You can't be a painter, or at least only an Impressionist like an exceedingly minor Van Gogh, if you're born as short-sighted as I am. You can't be a classical ballet dancer if you're born with flat feet. But if you're born with the good ear, the good eye, the high instep—then you're lucky.

Am I making it sound too simple? Oh, it isn't simple at all.

Talent has two faces. One is the face given by nature, that smiling smug brilliance of the child that is born on the Sabbath Day, and is fair and wise and good and gay. The other face is the one that the owner of the talent makes for it. That one isn't given at birth; it has to be won, and molded. I'm reminded of something George du Maurier once said—that until we are forty we have the face God gave us, and after forty we have the face we have made for ourselves.

The second face of talent is the one that matters. The term of highest praise in my vocabulary isn't *talented*—it's *professional*. That musician born with the good ear, he can't just sit back and make use of his talent only when he feels like it—if he's to develop, he must play and play and play. The dancer with the lucky high instep has to sweat for hours over ballet exercises at the barre. In the arts, if I may borrow an American phrase, nothing comes easy. Excellence certainly doesn't come easy. They say in ballet, that if you miss practice for one day you will know; if you miss two days your teacher will know; if you miss three days your audience will know. Every art demands dedication, and the dedication must be total.

As for writing: let me quote you something that has been a support of mine for the last thirty years. It was written by the English novelist Pamela Frankau. She said:

> The only way to learn to write well is to keep writing: the only way to safeguard the talent is to exercise it. And that means keeping the door of your room shut and working alone. Outside the door there may be the beguiling bandwagon noises, or the hollow silence of apparent defeat. Neither, as you work, is your concern. Your concern is with a gift and the service of it. Given the ready ear, the open eye, the purpose and the stamina, you will not be safe, because nobody can be safe. But you will be armed.

I like that. Especially when I'm listening to the hollow silence, sometimes. I would add to it one other quotation, from J. B. Priestley's autobiography, *Margin Released,* a passage to which I am so devoted that I keep copies of it ready-printed to send to aspiring young writers who ask for advice.

> Perhaps, as I have already suggested, it would be better not to be a writer, but if you must be one—then, I say, *write.* You feel dull, you have a headache, nobody loves you—*write.* It all seems hopeless, that famous "inspiration" will not come—*write.* If you are a great genius, you will make your own rules; but if you are not—and the odds are heavily against it—go to your desk, no matter how high or low your mood, face the icy challenge of the paper—*write.* Sooner or later the goddess will recognize in this a devotional act, worthy of benison and grace. But if what I am saying seems nonsense, do not attempt to write for a living. Try elsewhere, making sure the position carries a pension.

Professionalism is also a matter of acquiring the right assumptions, like the one that considers writing clean prose as much a part of good manners as knowing how to eat with a knife and fork. Professionalism is an assumption of hard work, of taking

17

endless pains. The professional goes to ridiculous lengths to satisfy his artistic conscience. He may spend a morning rewriting a sentence six times. He may read three months' work one day, dislike it, throw it out and start all over again. He may study some large boring tome for three solid days, to make one paragraph of notes which will back up a tiny reference in his new novel which nobody will notice.

For instance, in my last book, which isn't published as I write this, I have a time-slip in which one of my characters, a boy called Will Stanton, finds himself watching a group of ghostly people living a few moments of their lives in a century some three thousand years before his own. While I was writing the scene, one of these ghostly people came into my head as a woman dressed in a white robe, wearing round her neck a string of bright blue beads. I must have checked through at least a dozen reference books before I could make sure that I could keep her. Eventually I found that yes, textiles and weaving and bleaching techniques *were* sufficiently advanced at that point in the Bronze Age for the woman to be wearing a white robe. And yes, blue faience beads of the Egyptian type *were* found in burial mounds in Britain, dating from 1550 B.C. onwards, so she could have her string of blue beads. It was all pretty unnecessary, I suppose; I could have let the picture from my imagination go, without checking its basis. It really wasn't terribly likely that even the brightest thirteen-year-old reader would stop, cry "Aha!", and rush to the *Encyclopaedia Britannica* to check up on Bronze Age beads, instead of getting on with the story. But all the same it did matter, because *I* knew. If I hadn't checked every smallest detail as well as I possibly could, my conscience would have nagged me every time I turned to that page.

I have here to make a confession, related once more to the arrogance that can lurk behind a polite and diffident English façade. Inside me, and deep down inside every professional writer, there is a rude, opinionated craftsman, with steel-hard standards and an unchristian contempt for anyone rash enough to question them. Some years ago I wrote a book called *The Grey King*: a fantasy, set in North Wales, fourth in a sequence of five novels called *The Dark Is Rising*. I have in my file on this book two long letters, an exchange between author and editor. I must make it clear that this is not my beloved American editor, Margaret McElderry, with whom I seldom fight except over the eccentricities of my punctuation. This is another lady, then children's book editor at my English publishers. I'll quote you a few bits from the letters to give you a glimpse of two professionals sparring. I would describe the two as a picky editor and a determined author, but that might sound biased.

"On page 4 line 10," wrote the editor to me, "you say 'two men in the navy-blue railway uniform argued earnestly in Welsh.' Your description of railway uniform as navy-blue suggests that this is a feature particular to Wales rather than to the country as a whole. I don't think it is a detail that British readers would expect to have pointed out to them."

I wrote back, "The uniforms are described as navy-blue to give an image of two men in navy-blue uniforms. I have a weakness for color. None of the other five British people who have read the book has thought this point odd, so I think perhaps you are outnumbered."

The editor was not to be deterred. She was much possessed by the fact that I live in the United States, and must therefore have forgotten everything I ever knew about Britain. She wrote, "On pages 8, 50, 147 and 212 you refer to a Land Rover as 'small.' This suggests that you are thinking of a jeep, mini-moke or possibly Range Rover, which are all smaller, though less common in the farming districts of Wales. By British standards the Land Rover is a large vehicle, more like a utility truck than a car, with a much higher chassis and more horsepower than the average British car."

(If you thought blue beads from the Bronze Age were obscure, get a load of this.)

I wrote back, "Rubbish. I have been driving a Land Rover for six years. It is the short wheel-base Land Rover, 88 inches, as most are in North Wales due to the terrain, and it is smaller than a jeep and *half* the size of a Range Rover. (You are no doubt thinking of the long wheel-base Land Rover, more common in the South of England.) The Land Rover in the book, like mine, has a four-cylinder engine, is *far* smaller than 'a utility truck,' and certainly does not have 'more horsepower than the average British car.' "

The editor was not deflected one bit. She went on for pages, suggesting that I should check all sorts of points that I had already checked five times over and been long satisfied with. "On page 158 you have the boy Bran out on a bicycle expedition wearing a school cap," she wrote. "A knitted bobblecap is the most usual type of headgear for country boys."

I wrote back, with my teeth clenched, "I hope you don't seriously expect me to change this to 'bobblecap.' "

"The hyphenated word *creaky-neat* on page 53 is an American expression," the editor wrote. I wrote back, "I am fascinated to learn that *creaky-neat* is an American expression, since no American of my acquaintance has ever heard of it. This is not altogether surprising, since I invented it. This partiality for doubled adjectives is probably the only characteristic I share with Shakespeare, and is not going to change."

The nearest thing to explosion point came at one of the climaxes of the book, where I had an anguished Welshman called Owen Davies exclaim "Iesu Crist!" which is the Welsh for Jesus Christ. The editor wrote, "According to my Welsh adviser, the expostulation 'Iesu Crist' is a much more serious blasphemy in Welsh than in English, and not a very likely one for a chapel deacon to use, even under supreme stress. 'O'r nefoedd' has been suggested as being more appropriate—literal translation, 'from the heavens.' "

I wrote back, with great self-control, "Yes, 'Iesu Crist' is a serious blasphemy. That is why Owen is using it. Yes, it is an unlikely one for a deacon to use; that is also why he is using it. I am tempted to use it myself, at this stage . . ."

The blasphemy stayed in the book. I stayed with the same publishers. But only just. People who try to question the private standards of a rampant professional are playing a perilous game. It's a little like standing too close to a blacksmith when he's whacking at a white-hot horseshoe. (When the horseshoe cools down, of course, all is well. Under normal circumstances I was fond of my English editor, and the next time I was in London, we met very amiably for lunch. I even felt slightly guilty, though perhaps only because she was paying for the lunch.)

You may have begun to wonder by now what this kind of general discussion of the talent and craft of writing is doing in a conference concerned with children's books. In all this while I've only mentioned the phrase *children's books* twice, in passing. That's deliberate. Children's books, from the writer's point of view, are simply books which happen to be published on the children's list.

Obviously there are some specific aspects of children's literature which can't be discussed in the same terms as literature in general, otherwise there wouldn't be such things as children's lists. But the common ground between every kind of book is far more important. Literature is literature, whoever it's published for. *Sub specie aeternitatis,* when we're all dead, *Huckleberry Finn* will remain a literary classic just as reputable as *David Copperfield; The Water Babies* just as much as *Silas Marner; Wind in the Willows* just as much as *Vanity Fair.*

If we are trying to estimate the excellence of a work of art, we must use terms that apply to all works of art in that field. We are being unfair to children if we assume that their literature deserves anything less. As Lillian H. Smith said in that very good book of criticism *The Unreluctant Years,* "Children's books do not exist in a vacuum, unrelated to literature as a whole. They are a portion of universal literature and must be subjected to the same standards of criticism as any other form of literature."

21

The authors of books for children certainly don't exist in a vacuum; most of them think of themselves simply as authors. When John Rowe Townsend interviewed twenty children's writers for his book *A Sense of Story*, he said, "I didn't find a single one of them who would admit outright that he or she wrote specially for children." And Nicholas Stuart Gray, an Englishman who writes very good plays for children, was magnificently honest when interviewed for another book. He didn't write for children, he said: he wrote to make sure that the theater would have new audiences. "I'm not the slightest bit interested in children," said he. "I don't like them—or at least a lot of them. It was just that if the theater is going to exist, where are you going to start? If you are going to throw away children on films and television, then the theater itself is going to go down the drain."

I suppose most of us who write children's books do like children, especially if we have some of our own at home. But it doesn't follow. When I wrote my first children's book at the age of twenty-five, I hadn't even met a child for years—perhaps not since I stopped being one myself. Perhaps I have never quite stopped being one myself. Perhaps that's the only quality that's peculiar to writers published for children. Somewhere in our heads, somehow, there is retained the strange intuitive immediacy that the creative imagination shares with the alert, unjaded mind of a reading child.

Children of course make the best of all audiences for a writer. The child's reaction to a book is uncomplicated. He isn't uncritical or indiscriminating—indeed he's often harder to please than an adult. But his reaction to a book he likes is a little like falling in love. He gives it surrender, acceptance, a warm generous responsiveness—and an unselfconscious sense of wonder. It's very much indeed like the sense of wonder that the writer has, sometimes, at the best moments during the long slog of writing. You're sitting at the desk, in the middle of writing a passage whose shape you know only roughly, without being sure of every detail that's going to happen. And all at once, through that blessed door that leads into your thoughts from your unconscious mind, the imagination lets out some incident or idea that fills you with surprise and delight. And you think, "Yes! That's beautiful! That's just right!"—and you're off, scribbling. It's a kind of magic. You can't make it happen. You can only marvel when it does.

And perhaps it's in that, for children's books especially, that the hope of reaching this elusive thing called excellence hides. You need the two faces of the talent: the gift that's inborn, and the professional craft and technique that are practiced for so long that they become habit. But beyond that you need—a kind of magic. Some sense of wonder in your own imagination must link with that in the mind of the reading child. If any of us manages to produce something which the world labels excellent, it's because in the last resort we've found ourselves able to work that spell. It's a good word, *spell*. As Professor Tolkien pointed out, we shouldn't forget that *spell* in the old days meant not only a formula of power over living men, but also a story told. We writers can be proud of our hard work—if we work hard. But we can't be proud of that gift of spellbinding, only grateful for it. We have it only through a very large piece of luck.

Take Them to the Theater

An article written for Parents Choice, *1979*

Watch the child reading a book: *really* reading, totally caught up in the world into which the words on the page have transported him or, of course, her. He is sprawled or curled or propped in some inelegant position, face concentrated and intent, motionless; he isn't with you any more. He doesn't hear when you call; he doesn't notice that the sun has set and that he should turn on the light. He's away out there with the author, in wonderland.

Watch the child in front of the television set. He may be frozen in that same kind of rapture, but it isn't likely. If his eyes are intent on the screen, they have a faintly glassy quality; like the hypnotist, that TV sitcom has not captured all the powers of his thinking mind, but has put him into a trance. And if the trance is only intermittent, you can see that the screen has no firm hold on his conscious mind at all; he will chatter, fidget, get up to fetch a drink of water, come back. He's being entertained, but he is not caught up in a sense of mystery. The emotions he is feeling do not include wonder.

You've seen your child reading, and you've seen him watching television. But have you ever taken him to the theater?

If you have, and do, then you already know which of the two

descriptions above is closer to the experience of theater, and you need read no further. But if you haven't, I hope you'll stay with this article for a while.

Let us imagine a reasonably typical middle-class American couple whom we'll call, with striking originality, John and Mary. They have two children aged nine and twelve. They are literate and lively-minded; they buy books; they and their children watch television, but with discrimination. When John and Mary go out for an evening it is generally to a concert or to the theater; they belong to the Theater Guild, and look forward to the nights when they can settle the kids with the baby-sitter and the spaghetti and go off to the new show in town.

When they take the *children* out for an evening, they go to the movies, or for some special treat to the Ice Follies or the Nutcracker Suite ballet. It has never occurred to them to buy theater tickets instead. Why not?

"Well—there's always some movie that all their friends have told them to see."

"The theater would bore them."

"They're too young."

"There are so few plays suitable for children. I mean, sex, language, violence—at least movies have a rating to tell you in advance."

"And the *price* of a decent theater seat these days! If we all four went, that would be sixty bucks gone before you even turn around. How often can you afford to do that?"

Well, John and Mary, you could afford to try it once, at any rate. There are many things in the theater besides the shows chosen by the Theater Guild. In most cities you can find some valiant and dedicated repertory group, and wherever you may be during the summer vacation you are likely to be within reach of summer stock. The acting may not be of Broadway standard, but neither will the prices. If your children are very young you would probably be wise to look for "children's theater," though this is an unpredictable genre whose quality varies as widely as any single year's output of children's books. But if the children are ten years old or up, just *take them to a play.*

I can give you two good reasons, and the first has to do with the imagination.

Like anyone else who has written a quantity of fiction, I suppose I can claim to have an active imagination—that treasure that we all hope our children will acquire. I owe mine to Fate, my genes, and to my parents, who believed in the value not only of books and music but of families visiting the theater *en bloc.* Glowing through forty years of memory there remains in my head the sense of magic, of being transported to another world, that came from evenings at that dotty English institution the pantomime; at romantic musicals, Gilbert and Sullivan operettas, at plays ranging from Shakespeare to *Peter Pan.* (*Peter Pan* has been an institution in my family ever since my grandfather took his seven children to the very first performance, in London. "Clap your hands if you believe in fairies!" cried Peter, with that fervor that makes sophisticates curl up like salted slugs, and Grandad clapped louder than anyone there. And at the end, as was his custom at performances of which he approved, he stood up in his seat shouting, "Bravo! Bravo!" and his embarrassed children tugged at his coat and hissed, "Dad! Sit down!")

The only mistake my parents made was in once taking my brother and me to the Royal Opera House at Covent Garden; *Aida,* sung in Italian, was not the best meat for a twelve-year-old, and I fell fast asleep during the last act. But even so, I remember too the splendor of the production, and of the opera house itself.

I was hooked on the theater, for life. By the time I was fifteen I was making a weekly pilgrimage to the nearest repertory theater, two bus rides away, to sit high up in a hard gallery seat—one-and-sixpence for the delight of discovering Congreve and *Charlie's Aunt,* potboilers and classics and the glittering words of Shaw.

Most of the books I have written for children are classified as "fantasy." I don't really know why they come out that way, but I fancy the theater is somewhere at the root of it all. In that moment when the house lights go down and the voices die to a murmur, there is the enchantment of all escape, all discovery: the knowledge that when the curtain goes up, there before us on the stage will be a different world, in which we shall live until the curtain goes down again. The audience then is like that image of the child reading: lost, transported to wonderland. The only difference is that here the wonderland is real, visible. Those aren't actors up there, if a play is really working; they *are* Rosalind, Prospero, Puck.

I believe passionately that children should be given the chance to experience this particular enchantment. If it leaves them cold—well, fair enough; the theater-going public is remarkably small even among adults, though again, I think it would be bigger if more people were, in that awful but useful phrase, "exposed to theater when young." I feel with particular passion that children should see Shakespeare on the stage, well performed, before the plays become permanently deadened for them by becoming no more than "set books" at school. That's the difference between a new-baked loaf of bread, and powdered bread crumbs.

Practice what you preach. Well—my own children first encountered Shakespeare when Kate was eight years old and Jonathan ten. Two actors of our acquaintance were spending the season in Stratford, Ontario, home of the best Shakespearean productions in North America; Hume Cronyn was playing Bottom in *A Midsummer Night's Dream* and Shylock in *The Merchant of Venice,* and his wife, Jessica Tandy, doubling Titania and Hippolyta in *A Midsummer Night's Dream.* I took the children to Stratford for two days; they were mildly enthusiastic at the prospect of seeing the work of The Bard, though Jonathan was privately more interested in the make of the car I rented, and Kate in feeding the birds on the River Avon.

Then, their first evening, they saw *A Midsummer Night's Dream.*

I don't think they moved, or took their eyes from the stage, from the moment it began. The acting was excellent, the production beautiful, all black and white and gold; the children fell about with laughter at the mechanicals, and cheered at the end. And the wiggling of the ears of Bottom's ass's head quite overtook their exclusive devotion to the birds and the car.

The next afternoon they saw a matinee of *The Merchant of Venice*. Hume had them brought to his dressing room during an interval to see the makeup change which would help age his Shylock from a sharp-witted merchant to a broken, vindictive old man. They watched his deft hands, fascinated. Yet this bit of privilege made no difference; reason couldn't overpower the imagination. In the next act, when Shylock, knife in hand, sketched out the areas of Antonio's chest from which he proposed to cut his pound of flesh, I felt Kate's hand slip into mine and hold on, hard.

After the performance the Cronyns offered me a baby-sitter so that the children could be amused while I went to see a Chekhov play that night. "We can't come, alas—we shall be doing the *Dream*."

Jonathan said, "You will? Tonight? Please couldn't we see it again?"

"You can't be serious."

"Oh yes *please*," Kate said.

So within hours of sitting through the matinee of *The Merchant of Venice* they were sitting through *A Midsummer Night's Dream* again, as totally absorbed as they had been the night before. And they quoted Bottom and Wall and Quince all the way home in the airplane, greatly to the surprise of the man in the next seat. Somehow I don't think my kids are going to be bored by Shakespeare when they meet him at school.

I was saying, John and Mary, that there are two good reasons for taking your children to the theater. The second reason has nothing to do with the imagination or with literary values; it has to do with behavior. No one who has ever sat among children at a Youth Symphony Concert, or at any variety of children's theater, can escape the awareness that the average American child has no idea how to belong to an audience. Nobody's ever taught him. The only kind of entertainment which he is accustomed to watching is television, during which he can roam about, talk, eat, chew gum or do whatever he likes. Even at the movies, he's able to chew noisily on popcorn. The screen can't answer back; it neither demands concentration nor requires (or, generally, deserves) respect.

So when you put this child of the TV audience into a theater he too will talk, fidget, rustle his program and tend to behave as though the live performers were a mechanical screen. You will be doing him (and all future audiences, actors and musicians) a great favor if you show him, in your company, something which deserves and demands his full attention and respect.

Please, John and Mary and anyone else, take your children to a play. You will be introducing them to a ritual, a mystery, which has been curiously necessary to man for two thousand years; answering a need which few other things in their lives can satisfy. What's more, watching them enjoy the play will double the pleasure you have from enjoying it yourself.

And don't worry about the language. When the Cronyns had finished their Stratford season, they came to Boston in a sad, funny, uninhibited play called *The Gin Game*. My children, by then aged ten and eleven, wanted to go.

"Perhaps you shouldn't bring them," Jessica said. "I mean—the language—"

I said to the children, swallowing embarrassment, "I'll take you to the play, but I have to warn you that you'll hear Aunt Jess saying *shit* and *fuck*."

"Oh Mum," they said with amused tolerance. "We've heard far worse than that in day camp."

Nahum Tarune's Book

A talk given at Simmons College in 1980

From a place halfway between innocence and experience, here is the beginning of a story.

In my rovings and ramblings as a boy I had often skirted the old stone house in the hollow. But my first clear remembrance of it is of a hot summer's day. I had climbed to the crest of a hill till then unknown to me, and stood looking down on its grey walls and chimneys as if out of a dream. And as if out of a dream already familiar to me.

My real intention in setting out from home that morning had been to get to a place called East Dene. My mother had often spoken to me of East Dene—of its trees and waters and green pastures, and the rare birds and flowers to be found there. Ages ago, she had told me, an ancestor of our family had dwelt in this place. But she smiled a little strangely when I asked her to take me there. "All in good time, my dear," she whispered into my ear, "all in very good time! Just follow your small nose." What kind of time, I wondered, was *very good time?* And *follow my nose*—how far? Such reflections indeed only made me the more anxious to be gone.

Early that morning, then, I had started out when the dew was still sparkling, and the night mists had but just lifted. But my young legs soon tired of the steep, boulder-strown hills, the chalky ravines, and burning sun, and having, as I say, come into view of the house in the valley, I went no further. Instead, I sat down on the hot turf—the sweet smell of thyme in the air, a few harebells nodding around me—and stared, down and down.

My title is "Nahum Tarune's Book," and anyone who recognizes that name will also recognize the passage above. The rest of you may wonder what on earth I am up to. Who is Nahum Tarune? An eighteenth-century preacher? A leathery old Maine fisherman? Perhaps an Elizabethan composer, some obscure acquaintance of John Dowland?

None of these. Nahum Tarune belongs in fact to one of the most remarkable books in the English language: Walter de la Mare's anthology of verse, *Come Hither*. I've had my copy of this wonder for thirty years and must have turned to it at least as many times each year—sometimes for solace, sometimes for sunlight, always with an emotion that I have never quite been able to define. *Come Hither* is my talisman, my haunting: a distillation of the mysterious quality that sings out of all the books to which I've responded most deeply all my life—and that I dearly hope, as a writer, I might someday, somehow, be able to catch. But the quality is as evanescent as a rainbow; it will never stay to be examined. It's a kind of magic, but not from books which are necessarily *about* magic—not at all. What is it?

I don't know, but it's high time I tried to find out.

To begin at the beginning: *Come Hither* is magical not simply because it's a wonderfully far-ranging collection of verse put together by a very remarkable poet, but because it has an introduction and a set of notes half as long again as the verse. That doesn't sound very promising, I grant you. But the notes are no ordinary notes. They are the musings of a full and most agile mind, which wanders over hill and dale instead of keeping to the narrow path of scholarship. You read, for instance, an early poem which is a kind of general wassail, entitled "Bring Us in Good Ale"—and you find as a note to it the engaging information that in 1512 the two young sons of the Earl of Northumberland were allowed for their daily breakfast "Half a Loif of houshold Brede,

31

a Manchet, a Dysch of butter, a Pece of Saltfish, a Dysch of Sproits or iii White herrynge"—and eight mugs of ale.

Or there's the note to Chaucer's lines about the month of May, when, as you will remember, "the foules singe/And . . . the floures ginnen for to springe." This transports de la Mare into five pages of beautifully random reflections about flowers, including the observation that Shakespeare never mentions foxgloves once in all his plays—though he names the rose fifty-seven times and the violet eighteen. The reason turns out to be that foxgloves dislike limestone and are rarely found in South Warwickshire. So that, says our editor, "it is possible . . . that Shakespeare when a child never saw a foxglove . . . and it is what we see early in life that comes back easiest later." (It is, indeed. And it is, I suspect, the root of what I'm talking about.)

Now, I don't know about you, but when I was reading scholarly editions of this and that at university, I was never blessed with footnotes like those. I love the idea of finding out, gratis and with total irrelevance, that Shakespeare never saw a foxglove (after all, think what he might have done with it in A *Midsummer Night's Dream*), and that two small boys had eight mugs of ale and a manchet for breakfast in 1512. As a result I can even report to you, from the *Oxford English Dictionary,* that a manchet is "a small loaf or roll of the finest wheaten bread."

Let me go back to the introduction of *Come Hither,* which is called "The Story of This Book." The boy, Simon, set out to find East Dene and instead came upon a house in a valley, at which he stared, down and down. And then he went down, to the house. Its name was inscribed in faded letters on the gateway: THRAE. It was an old, old house with embrasured windows, a round stone tower with a twirling weathervane, and a great overgrown garden. And an old lady lived there, called Miss Taroone.

Our boy came back to visit it again and again, growing bolder and going closer each time, and at length he met Miss Taroone and came to know her house with its multitude of rooms. He heard that she had once lived on another more ancient family estate called Sure Vine. He learned of some villages nearby called the Ten Laps, and was told that there was indeed a way to East Dene from this house—he would come to a Wall and would have to climb over.

But instead of going hunting for East Dene, he stayed to explore Miss Taroone's house. She was a strange, aloof old lady. The story goes on:

> She never said anything affectionate; she never lost her temper. I never saw her show any pity or meanness or revenge. "Well, Simon," she would say . . . "you are always welcome. Have a good look about you. Don't waste your time here. Even when all is said, you will not see too much of me and mine. . . . Sleeping, waking; waking, sleeping, Simon"; she said, "sing while you can."

Then Miss Taroone told the boy about Nahum Tarune: Mr. Nahum. He was never quite sure of Mr. Nahum's relationship to her, but only that she had raised and taught him and that he had grown up in this house. One day she took Simon to the round room at the very top of the old stone tower, Nahum's room, and left him free to look at everything in it. It was the kind of marvelous room that you find described in books quite often, so often that I suspect every writer secretly hankers after it—or perhaps it's an image of the inside of any artist's mind. It was not unlike Merlin's room in *The Sword in the Stone,* full of

> . . . odd-shaped coloured shells, fragments of quartz, thunderbolts and fossils; skins of brilliant birds; outlandish shoes; heads, faces, masks of stone, wood, glass, wax, and metal; pots, images, glass shapes, and what not; lanterns and bells; bits of harness and ornament and weapons. There were, besides, two or three ships of different rigs in glass cases, and one in a green bottle; peculiar tools, little machines; silent clocks, instruments of music, skulls and bones of beasts, frowsy bunches of linen or silk queerly marked, and a mummied cat (I think). And partly concealed, as I twisted my head, there, dangling in an

alcove, I caught sight of a full-length skeleton, one hollow eye-hole concealed by a curtain looped to the floor from the ceiling.

Every inch of space on the walls, in this cluttered room, was covered in pictures painted by the absent Mr. Nahum. Some were of Thrae, some painted in foreign parts; many were from his mind. " 'He has,' said Miss Taroone, 'his two worlds.' " Over and over, Simon would stare at the pictures, never quite understanding why each had a name and Roman numerals on the back—as, for instance, BLAKE: CXLVII. Then one day, in one of the many bookcases in the room, he found a certain book.

It was "an enormous, thick, home-made-looking volume covered in a greenish shagreen or shark-skin. Scrawled in ungainly capitals on the strip of vellum pasted to the back of this book was its title: THEOTHERWORLDE." Simon—or Walter de la Mare—tells us that the book was full of rhymes and poems, some with Mr. Nahum's thoughts on them jotted in the margin, or a piece of prose bearing on a particular poem. Some had illuminated capitals, some were queerly spelled, some had names and numbers which linked with the pictures on the walls. Day after day the boy read them, as they took his fancy, and he learned to hear the music of the words and to see those pictures in them which were not on the walls.

And he began to realize that even when Mr. Nahum's pictures were about real things and places and people, they were still only of the places and people that the words made for him in his mind. He had, that is, to *imagine* all they told. So what he read remained as a single clear remembrance, as if his imagination had carried him away, like a magic carpet, into another world. He realized that Mr. Nahum had chosen only those poems which carried away his own imagination like that. And since they called to Simon's imagination, too, as the fowler's whistle calls to the wild duck, he sat down to copy them out and to make his own book.

So this inconsequential but unforgettable story leads to the collection of verse and prose which is *Come Hither,* the book which has haunted me, as reader and writer, since I was fourteen

34

years old. And de la Mare's struggle to describe the *kind* of poems that he found in Nahum Tarune's book is my struggle to find out precisely what the quality is, in this book and others, which carries me so deeply into delight.

We never meet Nahum Tarune in the story of *Come Hither,* but he is all of us. Walter de la Mare has been playing with words. Nahum: *human.* Tarune: *nature.* Nahum Tarune is human nature. I don't really have the right kind of mind for anagrams, crossword puzzles, or word games, and I find allegory a very tiresome form; the more ingenious and convoluted, the more tiresome it becomes. But here, being biased I suppose, I find the parallels so deliberately clear that they have both charm and power. Thrae is the Earth, spelled, in effect, backward; Miss Taroone is Nature (Mother Nature, if you like); Sure Vine is the Universe; the villages called the Ten Laps are the Planets; and the ancestral home East Dene is Destiny.

It doesn't *matter,* all this; it doesn't affect the nature of what de la Mare is doing. But it does perhaps add a dimension to the way in which Miss Taroone speaks to the small boy she persists in calling Simon (or, perhaps, as a thoughtful friend of mine suggests, "my son"). " 'Remember,' she says, 'that, like Nahum, you are as old as the hills, which neither spend nor waste time, but dwell in it for ages, as if it were light or sunshine. Some day perhaps Nahum will shake himself free of Thrae altogether. I don't *know,* myself, Simon. This house is enough for me, and what I remember of Sure Vine, compared with which Thrae is but the smallest of bubbles in a large glass.' "

In the images of this story—in the old house set in its broad valley, with misted mountains all around and beyond them a glimpse of the sea, and in Nahum Tarune's great book that has in it all the best reading of a lifetime—I find something like a beckoning phrase of music, which sounds all too rarely but is wonderful to hear. Once upon a time I put such a phrase into a book of my own, as a recurrent herald of enchantment. Perhaps it was part of the *Come Hither* haunting.

What is it, the hearing of this music, the sense of being

35

bewitched? It's not a matter simply of recognizing greatness or great talent. It isn't, as the jargon has it, a value judgment. It's subjective, idiosyncratic; perhaps it has something to do with form. I have that kind of gut response to a late Mozart symphony rather than to a Bach concerto grosso; to a Turner or a Renoir rather than to the formalities of the Flemish school. My appreciation of each, that is, is different—just as one finds different kinds of pleasure in reading different kinds of books. The appeal of a biography is different from that of a lyric poem; the appeal of a so-called realistic novel different from that of a so-called fantasy.

I say "so-called" because I've never been happy with either classification; classifying means drawing lines, and I find it hard to draw a line between any one novel and another. That magical shiver of response—I can't justify it by genre. I remember feeling it certainly from the moment the children in *The Five Children and It* first come upon the Psammead, the ancient living creature suddenly emerging from the sand after its thousand years of sleep, and certainly from the moment Kay Harker in *The Box of Delights* first meets the old man Cole Hawlings and is given that dreadful, thrilling message, "The wolves are running." But I remember it too from the cocky malice of Alan Breck in *Kidnapped,* or from a biography in which Lord Nelson, ordered to retreat, put the telescope to his blind eye and remarked airily, "I do not see the signal." Any line that's drawn has to be instantly trampled down.

That shiver, that *frisson,* when I was growing up, came from legend, myth, and fairy tale and from a great deal of verse. My mother and my schools between them, thank God, sent poetry ringing through my head to leave most powerful echoes. I can't really tell you how many of the novels I read were "fantasies." There was most of Kipling—but the sum included his "realistic" short stories as well as *The Jungle Book; Kim* as well as *Puck of Pook's Hill.* (But perhaps *Kim* is a fantasy? Perhaps *any* novel is a fantasy, in the last analysis.) There was Elizabeth Goudge's *Henrietta's House,* if any of you remember it. There was

Masefield, of course, and E. Nesbit, but Dickens and Jack London as well—and Arthur Ransome, whose books are certainly fantasies in their convenient and magical abolition of grown-ups. I was born too early for most of the overt fantasy that children read—or adults analyze—today. I never chanced to read George Macdonald; Tolkien didn't write *The Lord of the Rings* until I was an undergraduate; and it was only after I'd written five fantasies of my own that I took off on a deliberate orgy of reading the masters of the last twenty-five years: Alan Garner, William Mayne, Lucy Boston, Ursula Le Guin, C. S. Lewis and the rest. Mind you, books like *Earthfasts*, *The Children of Green Knowe* and *The Owl Service* produce that same stab of joy whatever age the reader may be.

But for me, when young and growing, that lovely shock came primarily from three things which are not "books" at all: from poetry, as I've said; from radio, which was at its peak as an imaginative medium in England when I was between ten and fifteen years old; and, above all, from the theater. My mother tells me that I was first taken to the theater when I was about three—to that Christmas institution in England known as the pantomime. I sat there enchanted, she says, not a whit puzzled by our transvestite tradition in which the hero of a pantomime is played by a strapping girl and the hero's mother by a large hairy man. And when it was all over and the curtain came down, I sat unmoving in my seat, and I howled and howled. All the others left on their legs, but they had to carry me out. I couldn't believe that this wonderful, magical new world, in which I had been totally absorbed, had vanished away. I wanted to bring it back again. I suppose I've been trying to bring it back again, in one way or another, ever since.

It's horribly elusive, this same kind of sensation one has from certain books, poems, and works of art. Only the symptoms are easy to describe. The hair prickles on the back of the neck, and there is a hollowness in the throat and at the pit of the stomach— a great excitement that is a mixture of astonishment and delight.

It's a little like catching sight unexpectedly of someone with whom you are very much in love. And the delight when it swamps you is full of echoes, carrying you away, as de la Mare said, "as if into another world."

The expectation of this, the hope of it in spite of all previous disappointments, is something that possesses me, always, in that moment which is one of the most powerful I know: when you are sitting in a theater before a performance, and the lights go down, and there is a hushed, murmuring expectancy, before the cur-tain—if there is one—goes up. It never fails to bewitch me, even if the play to come is one I've seen ten times before—just as a book or a poem can bring the same delight even if you've read it ten times before. I'm hoping always, I suppose, that when the curtain does go up, I shall find again the same joy that I found and lost, and mourned so embarrassingly, when I was three. And now and again, I do.

Why is the feeling so much intensified in the theater? It must be because, given the right playwright, the right actors, and the right director—all linked together by a rare and peculiar kind of chemistry—that special delighting quality comes totally alive to a degree possible nowhere else. The fantasy is made real. The other world is *there,* before your eyes. You are caught up, while the play lasts, in a waking dream.

For, of course, a dream, a particular kind of marvelous glowing dream that may come only once or twice in a lifetime, is the epit-ome of the whole thing. It's small wonder that mystics, blessed with a dream so ecstatic that they call it a vision, feel that they have had a glimpse of Heaven. Out of that part of the mind that is not sleeping there can come an image so powerful that it is an experience—odd and meaningless in itself, but always leaving a very strong visual impression and a sensation of intense joy.

I had one of those dreams three or four years ago, for no reason at all. I dreamed that I was high up on the roof of a build-ing in a great city; roofs and towers and pinnacles stretched all around me, all of them golden, glittering in the light of a newly risen sun. In just one direction, instead of the shining gold, there seemed to lie a wide park with tall, spreading green trees rising out of an early morning mist, like islands out of a white sea.

I knew in my dream that I wanted very much to go down, toward the park, toward the trees. I looked about me on the roof but could see no way down. Then I reached out and touched a golden balustrade that ran round the edge of my roof; and the part that I touched fell away and became a kind of ladder, unfolding as it fell, the sound ringing out musically over the silent city: clang, clang, clang. I looked at it rather nervously, I remember, and then I took a deep breath and climbed down; and from the ladder I reached a sloping roof with crosswise ridges that gave purchase for the feet. And I went down that roof and came to a great sweeping stone stairway, grey and sparkling like granite, and I ran down the stairs faster and faster, toward the trees.

Then I woke up, without, of course, having accomplished anything in the dream—but with a feeling of such wonder and excitement that I lay there smiling for a while and then got up and found a pencil and paper and wrote it all down. I half expected to find the paper full of gibberish in the morning, but there was the dream: recorded, real.

I was working on a book at the time, and a few weeks later I came to a point in my story where two of my characters were to find themselves in a magical place called the Lost Land. That was an image—the Atlantis myth, I suppose—that had haunted me ever since I was very young. But I had no picture of it in my mind. I sent my two characters on their way there, but I had no idea what they would find when they arrived. Then I remembered the dream, and I put it into the book; put my two boys up on that strange golden roof high in the golden city, to come down from it as I had come down. And they did, and found all manner of things when they reached the trees.

The dream seemed to me to fit naturally there, but I haven't the least idea whether it really did. I never read the reviews of my books, through cowardice or arrogance or perhaps both, so I don't know whether some critic said that my golden city was a strikingly original concept or whether another decried it as ludicrous and irrelevant. Perhaps nobody said anything about it at all. I rather hope so—that would mean that the image did fit.

The image. It seems always to be an image of one kind or another, that sparks off this reaction of fierce delight. And images are the language of the poetic imagination. Perhaps that's the key to my slippery puzzle—for the poetic imagination is not limited to writing verse. I've known, as you have, undeniable poets who never wrote a rhyme or a metrical line in their lives. It's a quality of certain creative minds. Robert Bolt, in the introduction to his play *A Man for All Seasons,* reflected on the fact that he had used poetic imagery in the writing of it and that nobody had noticed. "I comfort myself with the thought," he said, "that it's the nature of imagery to work, in performance at any rate, unconsciously. But if, as I think, a play is more like a poem than a straight narration, still less a demonstration or lecture, then imagery ought to be important. It's perhaps necessary to add that by a poem I mean something tough and precise, not something dreamy."

And tough and precise is what, to go back to our beginning, the best books read by children have to be. That audience will settle for nothing less. A dream itself, while it's happening, is almost always singularly tough and precise, though incomplete. Certainly those words apply to every book I've mentioned, in this stumbling attempt to ferret out the roots of delight. The story is tough, the language is precise, and the whole work is clothed— noticeably or not—in imagery.

Lucy Boston once wrote, "I believe children, even the youngest, love good language, and that they see, feel, understand and communicate more, not less, than grownups. Therefore I never write down to them, but try to evoke that new brilliant awareness that is their world."

"That new, brilliant awareness"—only the poetic imagination can bring it back. The freshness of a child's vision of the world is what every artist strives to retain. That's what we're all after, painters and poets and composers and the authors of certain kinds of books. If we can capture it, if we can make our audience catch its breath, create that great stillness that comes over a visible audience at moments of pure theater—if we can do that just a few times in our lives, then we've done what we were put here to do. And the whole life of an artist, it seems to me, is captured at the end of Walter de la Mare's story of *Come Hither*. Perhaps that, in the end, is the reason why this story, like others of the same magical kind, can carry away the longing, striving adult just as it does the unwitting, rejoicing child. Listen now to the music, and the metaphor.

The small boy Simon falls asleep one night over Nahum Tarune's book, and he wakes in the grey morning light in the tower room, amongst all the pages and pictures and strange outlandish objects, with an "indescribable despair and anxiety—almost terror even" at the rushing thought of his own ignorance and unimportance. "I thought," he says, "of Miss Taroone, of Mr. Nahum, of the life before me, and everything yet to do. And a sullen misery swept up in me at these reflections. And . . . I wished from the bottom of my heart that I had never come to this house."

But then the sun rose, and in the light, everything that had seemed strange became familiar; and he stood up and stretched.

To this day I see the marvellous countryside of that morning with its hills and low thick mists and woodlands stretched like a painted scene beneath the windows—and that finger of light from the risen Sun presently piercing across the dark air, and as if by a miracle causing birds and water to awake, and so too was the world itself, and ever is. And somewhere—Wall or no Wall—was my mother's East Dene. . . .

In a while I crept softly downstairs, let myself out, and ran off into the morning. Having climbed the hill from which I had first stared down upon Thrae, I stopped for a moment to recover my breath, and looked back.

The gilding sun-rays beat low upon the house in the valley. All was

ESCAPING INTO OURSELVES

An article for Celebrating Children's Books: Essays on Children's
Literature in Honor of Zena Sutherland, *edited by*
Betsy Hearne and Marilyn Kaye, 1981

The legs turn toward the library, the hands reach for a novel.
Why? "Well, I read for pleasure, of course." Of course: But
what's the root of pleasure, the reason why anyone, child or
adult, reads fiction?

The reason, simply, is entertainment. The novel entertains by
offering refreshment, solace, excitement, relaxation, perhaps
even inspiration: an escape from reality. And the escape, in turn,
brings encouragement, leaving the reader fortified to cope with
his own reality when he returns to it. So I hear the slam of the
door sometimes as my twelve-year-old Kate, feeling the weight of
the world upon her slender shoulders, retreats into her room;
and I know that she will shortly be curled up there with a book—
and will, afterward, feel better.

In "realistic" fiction, the escape and the encouragement come
from a sense of parallel: from finding a true and recognizable
portrait of real life. In those pages we encounter familiar problems, but they're *someone else's* problems; involved but secure,
relaxing into the story, we watch while the other fellow copes. If
the ending is happy, we are reassured; even in a difficult world,

all may be well at last. If the ending is tragic, the ancient cathartic effect of pity and fear takes over and we are reassured just the same, by the courage or steadfastness or simple humanity of the hero/heroine. We small people enjoy reading—need to read—about big people; at one end of that scale is the newspaper gossip column, at the other the New Testament.

Comic novels, thrillers, biographies, romances all have the same kind of appeal. So does science fiction, which does unearthly things to space and time but is still realistic fiction at heart. In all such books the reader knows, beneath the suspense of the story, what to expect; the "straight" novelist will not tamper with the limits of human behavior, nor the science fiction writer cheat by changing the laws of thermodynamics. Their greatest charm is that they play an exciting game according to rules.

There is just one kind of fiction which differs from all these. Why does anyone read, or write, fantasy?

Fantasy goes one stage beyond realism; requiring complete intellectual surrender, it asks more of the reader, and at its best may offer more. Perhaps this is why it is also less popular, at any rate among adults, who set such store by their ability to think. Among small children, who have not yet begun to think much about the stories they hear, fantasy reigns supreme. No realistic story has yet attained the universal affection they give to fairy tale, except possibly, in the United States, *Goodnight Moon*—which is not a story at all, but a deceptively simple ritual. Very young children, their conscious minds not yet developed, are all feeling and instinct. Closer to the unconscious than they will ever be again, they respond naturally to the archetypes and the deep echoes of fairy story, ritual and myth.

But after that, learning begins, as it must; the child is launched on his long quest of understanding. As he discovers the world around him, and the books which show him that world, his tastes in reading veer naturally toward realism. Some children not only reach that point but stay there; shunning fantasy as "babyish," they grow up to become those adults who seldom read novels at all, and find their escape and encouragement from those other contemporary escapist phenomena, which range, as Ursula Le Guin once wryly observed, from television soap operas to "that masterpiece of total unreality, the daily Stock Market Report." But others, born with a different chemistry, go on seeking out fantasy all their lives, instinctively aware that so far from being babyish, it is probably the most complex form of fiction they will ever find.

And what do we, and they, find when we read fantasy? The escape and encouragement are there, for sure—but in a different form. This time, when we depart from our own reality into the reality of the book, it's not a matter of stepping across the street, or into the next county, or even the next planet. This time, we're going out of time, out of space, into the unconscious, that dreamlike world which has in it all the images and emotions accumulated since the human race began. We aren't escaping out, we're escaping in, without any idea of what we may encounter. Fantasy is the metaphor through which we discover ourselves.

So it is for the writer, too. Every book is a voyage of discovery. Perhaps I speak only for myself, perhaps it's different for other writers; but for me, the making of a fantasy is quite unlike the relatively ordered procedure of writing any other kind of book. I've never actually *thought*: "I am writing fantasy"; one simply sits down to write whatever book is knocking to be let out. But in hindsight, I can see the peculiar difference in approach. When working on a book which turns out to be a fantasy novel, I exist in a state of continual astonishment. The work begins with a deep breath and a blindly trusting step into the unknown; I know where I'm going, and who's going with me, but I have no real idea of what I shall find on the way, or whom I'll meet. Each time, I am striking out into a strange land, listening for the music that will tell me which way to go. And I am always overcome by wonder, and a kind of unfocused gratitude, when I arrive; and I always think of Eliot:

We shall not cease from exploration
And the end of all our exploring
Will be to arrive where we started
And know the place for the first time. . . .

One of our best "realistic" novelists (how I hate these labels—but there's no way around them) said to me once, cheerfully rude, "Oh, you fantasy people have it so easy, you don't know you're born. If there's a problem in your plot—bingo, you bring in a bit of magic, and the problem's gone."

No, no, no, fantasy doesn't work that way; anyone cherishing such theories is bound for trouble. If he (or she) tries to sail our perilous sea in such a ship, he (or she) is likely to end up with a book which maybe is beautifully written, hugely entertaining, full of bits of magic—but which somehow isn't fantasy. True fantasy is John Masefield's *The Box of Delights,* or Alan Garner's *The Owl Service:* books which cast a spell so subtle and overwhelming that it has overpowered the reader's imagination, carried him outside all the rules, before he has noticed what is happening. To some degree I doubt whether Masefield or Garner or the rest knew what was happening either; they simply heard the music, and employed all their very considerable talent to write it down. You can't write fantasy on purpose. It won't come when called. Like poetry, it is a kind of happy accident which overtakes certain writers before they are born.

In case I seem to be portraying those of us who write fantasy as The Chosen, I might add that all other specific gifts within the realm of fiction are just as slippery, just as arbitrary. Very few writers can sow their seed successfully in more than one or two fields. Once, when I was young and very poor, I decided to chase an instant income by writing short stories for women's magazines. This wasn't my favorite occupation, but I knew I could write, and—believing that therefore I could write absolutely anything—I did my best. The stories were uniformly terrible and not one of them was published. Wiser and less arrogant—and still poor—I went back to the kind of writing I was born to do: that is, to the limited range of ideas that my imagination would offer unbidden. And those writers with a different kind of imagination, hearing a different music, went on writing very good short stories.

An entry in one of my working notebooks reads: "We are all at the mercy of the quality of the imagination we inherit. The book can never be better than that."

A writer's notebooks are perhaps the best illustration (better in some ways than the books themselves) of the way his mind works. Some consist of detailed blueprints for books or plays, set out with mathematical precision; some are filled with discursive examinations of character, building up backgrounds which may never appear in the story but which show the writer getting to know the people he has made. My own notes are mostly cryptic and random, full of images, scattered with quotations and ideas which often seem totally irrelevant to the book in hand—though they weren't at the time. Rereading them, I have always again the *feel* of what it is like to write fantasy, though whether any of this can be communicated by the notes themselves I do not know.

This book is mountains and lakes and valleys, birds and trees, with the sea in the distance glimmering, waiting. The last book is the lost cantref off the estuary, the drowned land where the bells sound. The long sands, the open sea and sky; the dunes.

* * *

If you wear agrimony, you may see witches. And if you look into their eyes, you see no reflection of yourself. The scarlet pimpernel is a charm against them.

* * *

Names of fields in Hitcham: Great and Lower Cogmarthon; Upper and Lower Brissels; Homer Corner; Hogg Hill.

* * *

The sword comes from the drowned land.

* * *

The opening of doors. Wakening of things sleeping. Revealing of old things forgotten.

* * *

Don't forget: "The mountains are singing, and the Lady comes."

* * *

Bird Rock. The birds remember. It is the door.

* * *

The "brenin bren y Ganllwyd," the great king oak near Dolgellau, felled in the early 18th century. Bole contained 609 cubic feet, and above this towered four great branches, each long enough for a mill shaft.

* * *

Sandpipers run, and scoot off into the air, in pairs and tens and little flocks. One leads Will somewhere.

* * *

Triad from the 13th century Exeter Chronica de Wallia:

"These are the kingdoms which the sea destroyed. . . . The second kingdom was that of Henig son of Glannog; it was between Cardigan and Bardsey, and as far as St. David's. That land was very good, fertile and level, and it was called Maes Maichgen; it lay from the mouth (of the Ystwyth?) to Llyn, *and up to Aberdovey. . . .*"

* * *

The Doors come back, perhaps in Book Five.

* * *

In Welsh, "glas" can mean green as well as blue, silver, greyish-white and slate-colored. The Welsh word for "grass" is "glas-wellt" (lit. green straw).

* * *

"Three freights of Prydwen went we into it,

But seven came back from Caer Siddi."

The seventh is Arthur, and we never see him. No one does, but Merriman.

* * *

A sailor tattooed with a star between thumb and forefinger.

* * *

48

Bran/Herne/Arthur. Perhaps to the very last minute I shan't be sure whether he stays or goes.

* * *

Corona Borealis, the Crown of the North Wind, just dipping over the northern horizon at midsummer.

* * *

The sea level was changing in the fifth century, causing floods; same time as the Saxons were harrying the Romano-British. Irish invading too. In the peace of Arthur, the English had Sussex, Kent, Norfolk but not Bucks, Middlesex, Oxford. Twenty-one years between Badon, and Arthur dying at "Camlann." When does the Tree grow? Well—now, I suppose. Or outside Time.

* * *

At the last battle, Will glimpses all the lost faces: Owain, Gwion, the king. Even a girl throwing him a red rose. You never did use that red rose . . .

In the *Poetics* Aristotle said, "A likely impossibility is always preferable to an unconvincing possibility." I think those of us who write fantasy are dedicated to making impossible things seem likely, making dreams seem real. We are somewhere between the Impressionists and abstract painters. Our writing is haunted by those parts of our experience which we do not understand, or even consciously remember. And if you, child or adult, are drawn to our work, your response comes from that same shadowy land. Like us, you are escaping into yourselves.

I have been attempting definitions, but I am never really comfortable when writing about "fantasy." The label is so limiting. It seems to me that every work of art is a fantasy, every book or play, painting or piece of music, everything that is made, by craft and talent, out of somebody's imagination. We have all dreamed, and recorded our dreams as best we could. How can we define what we are doing? How can a fish describe what it's like to swim?

So having asked those questions, I sat in my study brooding hopelessly over a proper dispassionate description of the nature of fantasy, when I heard slow careful footsteps on the stairs. My daughter Kate came in, carrying a dish of water in one hand and some curious funnel-like instrument in the other. I said, "I'm stuck."

Kate smiled vaguely but ignored this, just as she had ignored the prohibition against Disturbing Mother at Work. She said, "Watch," and she dipped the funnel into the dish and blew through it, and out of the funnel grew the most magnificent bubble I have ever seen, iridescent, gleaming.

"Look at it from here," said Kate, intent. "Just look at the light!" And in the sunlight, all the colors in the world were swimming over that glimmering sphere—swirling, glowing, achingly beautiful. Like a dancing rainbow the bubble hung there for a long moment; then it was gone.

I thought: *That's* fantasy.

I said: "I wish they didn't have to vanish so soon."

"But you can always blow another," Kate said.

MORE LIGHT THAN DARKNESS

Graduation address given at Buckingham Browne & Nichols School,
Cambridge, Mass., June 1984

My children, Jonathan and Kate, went to school at Buckingham Browne & Nichols, a private school in Cambridge, Massachusetts, which was welded into a sturdy coeducational institution by a gifted headmaster called Peter Gunness after The Buckingham School (female) merged with Browne & Nichols School (male) in 1974. Cambridge being a fairly articulate community, BB&N has a policy of inviting a parent to be its graduation speaker, every second year. In the year Jonathan graduated, Peter invited me, and the piece that follows is the graduation address I gave. Rereading it, I am ruefully aware of its middle-class assumptions; even the poorest child in this privileged bunch was headed for college, and this wasn't the address you'd give to a graduating public-school class in Harlem or Watts. But I include it because it wasn't really about going to college; it was about growing up.

Even when most relaxed I'm not a self-confident speaker, but I've never been quite so nervous as I was on June 6, 1984. Here were 109 young people, and all their proud families, on a key day of their lives; if I said the wrong things, I should horribly embarrass both my children—Jon up there in the graduating class, Kate sitting with her flute in the school orchestra—in a way they would never forget. I was greatly a-twitch.

51

But it was all right. Graduations are such emotional occasions that perhaps you can't go wrong. I noticed a few gratifying hand-kerchiefs dabbing eyes in the audience as I finished, and I sat back in relief on one side of the stage as the new graduates were sum-moned one by one to receive their diplomas. When the roll call reached the name "Jonathan Roderick Grant," Jon paused halfway across the stage on his way toward the headmaster, and with the whole hall watching, came over to give me a kiss. And it was my turn to need a handkerchief.

Ladies and gentlemen of the Class of 1984:
One of the first things we find out about life, even before we graduate, is that we are all the victims of circumstance and geography. These past few days I have been discussing with my friends in the senior class how we might vanquish the eccentric geography of BB&N's gymnasium, which dictates that the grad-uation speaker shall deliver his (or her) address to an audience of graduates whom he (or she) can't see. We thought I might simply turn around, but since they sit up here on either side of me that doesn't really help much. Then we thought I might make my speech . . . like someone . . . watching a tennis game . . . saying one phrase to one side . . . and one to the other . . .

But in the end we accepted our side-to-side circumstance—because it has, after all, become part of the ritual.

And of course ritual is the name of today, of this Commencement, this ending which is a beginning. It has all the earmarks of ritual: a time-honored order of events; symbolic acts, like the giving of gifts and the passing of a torch; and a traditional final song, "Jerusalem," which perilously heightens emotion—particularly mine, since the song's all about England. All through life we seem to need these rites of passage: birthdays, marriages, funerals, graduations. They are breathing spaces in the busyness of living; they make us stop and think. You seniors here at my sides, you've all known you were leaving high school, but here today you face the fact of it, inescapable. The

52

moment's come; suddenly it's real. You'll walk across this stage, and Dad will give you your wings and push you out of the nest.

And we, the parents, have all known that our children were becoming young men and women—but here today we shall watch one particular figure, in that line of familiar and yet strangely grown-up figures going up to get their diplomas, and we may feel that we are looking at him or her for the first time. *Where in the world did the children vanish?* My graduating Jonathan held out his hand to me the other day (reaching perhaps for the salt, but more probably for the telephone), and I looked at it and saw a man's hand, scarred with those horrendous blisters that crewmen—and women—get from pulling an oar. And I thought: eighteen years ago that hand was only just big enough to hold one joint of my index finger. *Where in the world did the children go?*

Class of 1984, be patient with your parents. Even after this ritual, we're still going to remind you that curfew is such-and-such a time; that your clothes won't get washed if you leave them in that grotty heap on the floor; that yes, sure you can drive home from the party—but please don't drink. We shall probably still be saying those things when you're twenty-five. Habit dies hard. We go on like that because you are our investment in the future. I'm not talking about tuition fees—those belong to a basic economic fact: that if you want something good, you have to pay for it. You are our *emotional* investment. We produced you, most of us, for the reasons that I hope you will produce your own children: not out of miscalculation or absentmindedness, but because we felt that on the whole there was more light than darkness in the world. Having kids, in this uncertain age, is an expression of faith in tomorrow. It's a way of saying: I believe that the world need not blow itself up; that people *can* get along with other people, if we go on trying.

If *you* go on trying. We've watched you developing into the next generation to carry that hope, and the burden of trying to make things better. We've watched you laughing, wondering, sometimes suffering; we've watched you learning to cope with responsibility, and the impact of disappointment and divorce and even death. We have tried to help, though we know that sometimes nobody can help. And we are very, very proud of you. There have been occasions when we have wanted to beat your heads against the wall—and you know those in reverse, about us—but we love you a lot. When you are off at college, we are going to miss you quite dreadfully. For the first few days, you will miss us too; but after that, I hope, you will be too busy.

I suppose I have the honor to be standing here not only because I'm a proud parent, but because of what I do. I'm a writer: of books, plays, screenplays, you name it. A freelance artist. It is not an occupation of the kind your parents would wish for you. It is unpredictable, insecure and decidedly flaky. On one day of the year I may receive a check that makes my children think we should instantly buy a Rolls-Royce, and then for the next six months I shan't earn a penny. (It is during that six months, of course, that there comes the phone call about the BB&N Capital Development Fund.) My parents wanted me to be a lawyer, and I don't blame them. But I was born with a particular kind of imagination, and it pointed me to the life that I lead now. I wouldn't claim to be always happy—Georges Simenon once said that writing was not a profession but a vocation of unhappiness—but I'm certainly happier than I should be if I were doing anything else.

Some of you, graduating now from high school, know roughly the occupations in which you want to spend your lives—medicine, engineering, teaching, whatever—and some of you haven't the least idea. In the course of the next four years, you're going to find out. Don't decide too quickly. Be prepared to change your mind. Most of us, here in the BB&N family, live in communities which are preponderantly academic or professional: many of your mothers and fathers are teachers in schools or universities, lawyers, doctors, architects, engineers, executives in large corporations or entrepreneurs running their own smaller companies. Without any of these highly accomplished people putting any conscious pressure on you, you may instinctively feel that it's *that* range of careers from which you should eventually choose your way of life. And maybe that's true—but maybe, for some of you, it's not.

Listen, these next few years in college, for the voice of the talent or ambition that may begin to mutter for the first time, surprisingly, at the back of your head. Listen to your imagination. You're going to change, and grow, as you learn more. If you come across something that makes you feel: *I'd like to spend my life doing that*—no matter how unexpected it may be, breeding roses, building boats, teaching deaf children to speak—give the ambition a chance to grow. It's *your* life, and it only comes once. Have fun with it; make something worthwhile out of it. Yes, it will be nice if you can end up prosperous and successful, but these things are a side effect of hard work and good luck—I beg you not to make them your primary goal.

Build on the foundation that BB&N gave you: not just the education, but the values and the sense of service and the love of friends. Make the most of those years at college: There's a lot more available to you there than the courses you have to take, and I'm not just talking about the opposite sex. Yes, there's a social life, and yes, you'd better work at your courses, or you'll very rapidly be out on your ear. But I didn't develop into a writer at university just by learning to speak Anglo-Saxon, and writing a lot of heavy critical papers about Chaucer and Milton. Those things helped, I suppose, but so did editing the university newspaper, and writing short stories for university magazines, on the side. Use all the ways you can find, in that new community, to develop your talents and expand your imagination. *Belong* to the college, as you've belonged to BB&N. Remember, above all, that you will never again have so much time to talk and think and read and discuss. Never. *Use it.*

It's going to be hard work, and it's going to be fun. It's a great beginning. I envy you your Commencement.

So Godspeed to you, Class of 1984. Have a good summer. Drive carefully—please. And during the summer, as you grow further from school and closer to university, remember today, sometimes: this happy-sad ritual. It's the symbol of everything this special school has given you, and everything you've given the school. The memory is like a lucky piece that you can carry in your pocket, and hang on to when you need reassurance or comfort. And it will always be there. Because you'll never really leave BB&N, you know. You'll take it with you, where you go.

above the stage. The theater was dark; only that hovering room and its books were brightly lit, and the readers, absorbed, sat unheeding at their tables and read on.

And at that point, always, I woke up.

I dreamed this dream three or four times in a period of, I suppose, three or four years. Eventually, when I was writing the last book in my sequence, *Silver on the Tree,* I came to a point in my story where two boys walked through a door. I left them there, walking through, at the end of one writing day. I didn't know what they would find on the other side. The next day, when I began to write about what they saw, I found myself describing the strange library-theater of my dream—and I've never dreamed about it since. Perhaps it wanted a life of its own, a chance to get into other imaginations than mine, and was now content that it had been set free. For this of course is what happens to any character or place or image that a writer puts into a story: born in one imagination, he, she or it is then born again, over and over, in the separate imaginations of every reader of that story, until the last copy of the book falls apart or the last reader forgets. No wonder Tolkien called storytelling "sub-creation."

My dream itself had the usual echoes in it of the past, present and future of the dreamer. All my life I had been rooted in libraries, both as a reader of other people's books and writer of my own. All my life I had been stagestruck, haunted by the theater. Within a year of finishing *Silver on the Tree* and my sequence of novels, I was writing scenes for John Langstaff's *Christmas Revels* at Sanders Theatre in Cambridge and beginning to collaborate with the actor Hume Cronyn on a play called *Foxfire,* which eventually made its way to Broadway. The wall of the library had melted away, and I was down in the theater which had been waiting beyond. I've been moving between the two ever since.

But if we detach that little dream from personal experience, it can be a useful metaphor of another kind. Take a man or woman at an early age, in the condition which is known as childhood, and put him or her into a library. Give the child a book to read.

(I am using my library to stand for any nook or cranny in which a child may read, from the bedroom to the subway, from the breakfast table to—well, the library.) Once the child's imagination is caught up in that book, particularly if it deals with experiences beyond his own world, beyond reality—then boundaries vanish, walls disappear, and he finds himself facing a wonderful space in which anything can happen. He's transported into my dream theater.

The theater. Consider the image. A magical place, quiet and dark most of the time—sometimes for months on end, if its owner is unlucky—but a place which once in a while is brilliant with light and life and excitement. It lies there sleeping, closed up, its doors all locked—until suddenly one day the doors are open and you can go in, and find wonder and delight. That isn't a bad image of the unconscious mind.

Fantasy, our subject and my preoccupation, comes from and appeals to the unconscious. It draws all its images from that dark wonderland, through the mysterious catalyst of the creative imagination. Nobody has ever described the process better than that great librarian, Lillian H. Smith, in her book *The Unreluctant Years*. "Creative imagination," she said, "is more than mere invention. It is that power which creates, out of abstractions, life. It goes to the heart of the unseen, and puts that which is so mysteriously hidden from ordinary mortals into the clear light of their understanding, or at least of their partial understanding. It is more true, perhaps, of writers of fantasy than of any other writers except poets that they struggle with the inexpressible. According to their varying capacities, they are able to evoke ideas and clothe them in symbols, allegory, and dream."

Symbols, allegory and dream. Like ritual and myth, those other mighty ancestors of fantasy, they have in recent years been much more widely discussed than is usual in this country, thanks to the television journalist Bill Moyers. First, public television gave us *Moyers: Joseph Campbell and the Power of Myth*, Moyers's six one-hour interviews with the mythologist Joseph Campbell, and then Doubleday published what I suppose would be called the book of the series, *The Power of Myth*. The interviews were watched by two and a half million people, and the book was on *The New York Times* best-seller list for six months. Between them they made Campbell's ideas far more accessible than his own books had done over the last forty years; he was a good writer but a better teacher, and *The Power of Myth,* both on film and on the page, is captivating.

When Joseph Campbell talks about myth, he is talking about the tree of which fantasy is a branch—or more accurately, a whole cluster of branches. And his great complaint is that we live today in a demythologized world: a society without the guidelines of ritual, a society which lacks the unconscious awareness of long-established patterns of civilized behavior, and falls into destructive violence as a result. The United States, says Campbell, has no ethos. *Ethos* had me reaching for my dictionary, because to me it meant character, and you could hardly accuse the United States of having no character. In the *Oxford English Dictionary* I found a more specific meaning, deriving from Aristotle on Rhetoric: "The characteristic spirit, prevalent tone of sentiment, of people or community; the 'genius' of an institution or system." So, back to Campbell. The United States, he says, has no ethos: as a vast jumble of people from different nationalities and traditions, it lacks the web of assumptions about social behavior that you find in a deep-rooted homogeneous culture— "an unstated mythology, you might say." Instead it is held together by law. Our children in America share with all mankind a deep and ancient hunger for myth, but there are no myths for them to inherit—so some of them make up their own. "This is why we have graffiti all over the city," says Campbell. "These kids have their own . . . morality, and they're doing the best they can. But they're dangerous, because their own laws are not those of the city."

He is talking only about a particular stratum of urban youth, but there is no question that we live in the most violent society in the so-called civilized world. One statistic will do. In one year—1990—the number of people killed with handguns in Japan was eighty-seven; in Sweden, thirteen; in Australia, ten; in Canada, sixty-eight. In Great Britain, the total was twenty-two. The population of the United States is four times as large as that of Great Britain. Multiply the British figure by four and you get eighty-eight. But the number of people killed with handguns in the United States that year wasn't eighty-eight; it was 10,567.

For Joseph Campbell, this is the violence of a cultural chaos; a civilization without mythological foundation. Myths are "stories about the wisdom of life," he says. "What we're learning in our schools is not the wisdom of life. We're learning technologies, we're getting information." Whenever he lectured, he says, he found a real hunger in his students, because "mythology has a great deal to do with the stages of life, the initiation ceremonies as you move from childhood to adult responsibilities . . . the process of throwing off the old [role] and coming out in the new."

He says: "[Myths] are the world's dreams. They are archetypal dreams, and deal with great human problems. I know when I come to one of these thresholds now. The myth tells me about it, how to respond to certain crises of disappointment or delight or failure or success. The myths tell me where I am."

The myths tell me where I am. Fantasy tells me where I am.

Perhaps I shouldn't use these two words interchangeably, in this context, without justifying what I am doing. Joseph Campbell, as you might expect, is eloquent in defining myth. "A dream is a personal experience of that deep, dark ground that is the support of our conscious lives, and a myth is the society's dream. The myth is the public dream and the dream is the private myth. . . . Myth must be kept alive. The people who can keep it alive are artists of one kind or another. The function of the artist is the mythologization of the environment and the world."

He's saying that artists have inherited the myth-making function of the shaman and the seer, and of course he's right. Where the art of writing is concerned, his point applies most of all to the poets and the writers of fantasy. Both deal with images, and with their links to and within the unconscious mind. And the fantasist—not one of my favorite words—deals with the substance of myth: the deep archetypal patterns of emotion and behavior which haunt us all whether we know it or not.

All of us who write fantasy are creating, in one way or another, variations on a single theme: We have a hero—or heroine—who has to cross the threshold from his familiar world into the unknown. In search of some person or thing or ideal, he has a series of adventures, undergoes trials, survives dangers and disasters, until he achieves his goal, his quest. And having achieved it, he comes home again a wiser person, better prepared for the longer journey which is now ahead of him, the adventure of living his life.

This is not a blueprint which every writer deliberately follows: God forbid. Indeed many try assiduously to keep away from it. But when you look back over a book of genuine fantasy, you can always see the pattern lurking inside it, in however shadowy a form. The echo of myth runs through fairy tales and folk tales from every culture, every tradition; in our own literature it runs through *Pilgrim's Progress* to *Gulliver's Travels, Alice's Adventures in Wonderland* to *The Wizard of Oz*, from Macdonald to Tolkien, from Lewis to Le Guin. When I look at my own books, I see a continual reiteration of the quest theme; not only in the *Dark Is Rising* books and my other fantasy novels, *Seaward* and *Mandrake*, but even in the nonfiction. I wrote a book called *Behind the Golden Curtain* which was, now I come to think about it, my personal quest in search of the nature of America; I wrote a biography of the English author J. B. Priestley which spent much of its time portraying him as a man in search of his own lost youth. And as I reflect on the book I'm writing now, I can see it is already taking on the pattern of a leaving and a search, to be followed no doubt (though I haven't the least intention of this at the moment) by a return. I am clearly stuck: so deeply imbued with the archetypes of fantasy and myth that I can't write about anything else. Well, I'm in some good company.

It is quite possible that I *need* these archetypes, not just as an artist, but personally. After all, writers are at the mercy not only of the quality of imagination they inherit, but the quality of character that came along with it. What is certainly true is that certain *readers* seem to need that archetypal pattern.

The children who write to authors of fantasy novels fumble to explain why they like such books, and come up with sentences like these from my own mail. From a thirteen-year-old in Texas: "Your books are my escape from the world I live in. I often wish I were one of the Old Ones, fighting the Dark and protecting Mankind from harm." A thirteen-year-old in Britain: "When I open your books I feel myself slipping out of this world and into another. I am one of those people who long for Adventure, and reading your books is the closest I have ever come to being in one." From a twenty-year-old in Illinois: "You give all of us the chance to leave the mundane struggles we face and enter a slightly grander struggle for a while." A sixteen-year-old in Sweden: "I get such a feeling when I read your books. It's like I want to climb up to the pages and walk straight into it and help Will and his friends." And from a twelve-year-old in Britain, the simplest and perhaps the most accurate: "Your books seem to fit me just right."

All of us need adventure, though of course it's easier to handle vicariously, through the pages of a book, than when it actually arrives. The celebrated cathartic effect, that mixture of pity and fear which is supposed to refresh the soul, is better acquired by watching *King Lear,* or reading about him, than by actually being King Lear. Just consider being King Lear. You have two psychotic daughters who murder each other, your best friend has his eyes torn out, and you go raving mad on a stormy heath, and end up dying of a broken heart with your third daughter's body in your arms. A memorable life, but not an enjoyable one. Fantasy, unlike real life, offers amazing adventures with no price tag; all you have to do is open a book. And afterwards, if one of its adventures does ever happen to overtake you, somewhere in your unconscious mind you will be equipped to endure or enjoy it.

We all need heroes, too, and not only when we're children. In story, in myth, the hero may die, but he must be replaced. The king is dead; long live the king! Among the few societies which still keep this pattern alive, Great Britain is a fortunate country; there is a great deal to be said for constitutional monarchy. The actual governing is all done by a democratically elected Parliament; the monarch has no power at all, but leads a benevolent and very public life as a figurehead, a focus for ritual and emotion—a hero. Popularity is less important for a British prime minister than for an American president, since in Britain the public can focus all its adoration, all its hero-worship, upon the Queen—not to mention Prince Charles, Princess Di, and the younger Royals, who continue to attract huge attention despite behavior which is far from regal. The allure of royalty even spreads beyond national boundaries, to wistful millions in kingless, queenless countries: When Charles and Diana were married in 1981 it was estimated that the wedding was watched on television by an eighth of the population of the globe. And despite the merciless spotlights that shine ever more brightly on his unfortunate private life, if Prince Charles ever manages to succeed to the throne, he will instantly acquire new stature; through the ritual of the coronation, the magic of monarchy, he will become a new worldwide hero.

We are short of such figures in the United States. (I take the liberty of saying "we" even though I'm not an American, because I have after all lived here for twenty-five years.) We have rich and powerful men and women; we have people of great talent and intelligence or beauty, or all three—but where are the figures to attract that deep, worshipful fervor drawn out by the mystique of the ritual hero? Who are *our* heroes? Ronald Reagan? Donald Trump?

There have been figures with the stature of heroes: John Fitzgerald Kennedy, Martin Luther King, Jr. But they're dead,

64

assassinated, and their stature has been vastly increased by the fact that they did die, as if they were powerful images of ritual sacrifice. They died, but they weren't replaced. Today, in general, we don't have heroes; we have celebrities—people well known not for their gigantic accomplishments but simply for being well known. Joseph Campbell was appalled by the results of a questionnaire which was sent around a high school in Brooklyn, asking the students, "What would you like to be?" Two-thirds of them ticked off the answer: "A celebrity." They didn't aspire to achievement, Campbell unhappily noted; they wanted simply to be known, to have name and fame. It's small wonder, with this scale of values in place, that we have such depressing presidential elections, with the candidates judged less by their ability or potential or beliefs than by their charisma, their image—or lack of it.

This is a very, very young country. Yes, we need outlets for mythic adventure, and we need mythic heroes. But you can't expect development that in other lands took three thousand years to be accomplished here in less than three hundred. The history of England, for instance, is a long layering of different traditions, as one culture after another came invading the island and taking control from the one which had invaded last time. There were lots of invaders, and each *one* of them lasted at least three hundred years. The English have ended up as an extraordinary interbred mix of Pict, Celt, Angle, Saxon, Jute, Dane, Roman, Norman—but time has merged all those different elements into a kind of rich compost, out of which an unmistakably English character and way of life slowly grew. America, now— America is an extraordinary mix of English, Italian, Irish, German, Scandinavian, African, Polish, Japanese, Chinese, Spanish, Russian, West Indian—you name it. But they haven't blended; they haven't had enough centuries; and the first invaders (who came from England) didn't even try to blend with the culture that was here before them—instead they did their level best to destroy it. The myths and imagery of the Native American could have become as potent a basis for this country's cultural development as the classical and Celtic myths were for Western Europe—but that didn't happen, and now it can never happen. The nation had to grow too fast; there wasn't time—and there certainly isn't time now. Almost every one of the older nations of the world has a slow-grown mythological foundation: what Campbell called its own ethos. The United States, instead, has a gap.

I think perhaps that the task of fantasy, in our contemporary world, is to help fill that gap.

Our society itself tries to fill the gap, without knowing it, but it does so from the wrong end; it tries to put in a foundation by stuffing things into the attic. Let me digress, in order to explain.

When I first came to this country in 1962, as a wide-eyed young newspaper reporter, I was hit very hard by two over-whelming impressions. The first was wonderful; it was the sense of opportunity, "anybody can do anything"—the sense of freedom that always enraptures visitors from England's comparatively rigid structure of tradition and behavior. The second impression was less wonderful, but fascinating: a more gradual realization that this freedom-loving society was gripped by a longing for ritualization. It began from the moment I stepped off the air-plane in Washington; the first thing I saw, after the startling glimpse of policemen wearing real guns, was a line of about twenty-five teenage girls all dressed as Little Bopeep, marching through the airport, chanting. I said to my American escort, "*What's that?*" He looked slightly embarrassed and he said, "Oh, they're from a sorority. That's something they have to do, to join it. A kind of initiation rite."

I'd never heard of Joseph Campbell then.

Fraternities and sororities, like the Elks and Kiwanis and the Sons of Italy, the golf clubs and the country clubs—they all thrive on rituals of membership. Then there's American football, an amazing ritualization of the relatively simple game of rugby. The players no longer wear simple shorts and shirts; they are all decked about with special helmets and padding, as ceremonially armored as medieval knights approaching a joust. They huddle together to murmur ritual numbers to one another; they launch into a sequence of ritual movements—and then someone waves a flag or blows a whistle, and they all stop, in order that the ground may be ritually measured and the ceremony start all over again. During any pause, groups of nubile young women leap in unison beside their team, and chant ritual chants to the god Ra (as in Rah! Rah! Rah!). At a central break in the ceremony, another group of acolytes moves in stylized patterns over the sacred ground, playing musical instruments, while a priest figure makes ritual motions with a sacred stick. On particularly sacred dates all this may be watched by as many as one hundred million people on small ritual boxes containing a glass screen.

Other kinds of ritualization are more insidious, based on the second of the two founding principles of the United States: freedom, and the right to make a profit. There are no longer any sacred festivals in the American calendar, religious or otherwise; there are only celebrations of commerce, filling the stores with Christmas goods in October and turning Thanksgiving into the year's biggest buying weekend. Eighty-five percent of the load carried by the average American mailman consists of ritual pieces of paper exhorting folk to spend money. Alternatively, they ask them to give money away. Charities have adopted the complex and manipulative ceremonies of advertising—and so have senators, who reach their positions of power not simply by free elections but by raising an average of three million dollars for their election campaign—ten thousand dollars for every week of a six-year term. The only known exception has been Senator William Proxmire of Wisconsin, who claimed to have spent on his last election campaign in 1982 a total of $145.10, all out of his own pocket. And he won.

The newest and fastest-growing ritual imposed on modern life is that of the computer, whose complex ceremonial amounts to a new secret language and way of thinking. *The Power of Myth* rehearses the story of President Eisenhower, confronted with the first major computer complex and told that he can ask it any question he pleases. The president eyes the machine and asks, "Is there a God?" And the lights flash, and the wheels turn, and after a while a voice says, "*Now* there is."

The computer is an Old Testament God, says Joseph Campbell, with a lot of rules and no mercy. I think of that every time I try to communicate with my Macintosh and it shows me a small frowning face, or says, like the Mad Hatter, "No Room!"

The kinds of ritualization I've been contemplating here are those which a society unconsciously imposes on itself out of a deep, unwitting sense of need. But they can't satisfy the need. Instead they produce phenomena like those high-school children whose dream was not heroism, not achievement, but celebrity. Underneath, there is still the gap—down there in civilization's basement, in the collective unconscious. If fantasy is the only thing with a chance of filling the empty basement of what Campbell calls "our demythologized world," what are its chances of success?

It would be nice to be able to say: Let's make all the children in the country read more, and let's introduce more of them to fantasy. Make sure curricula and reading lists are full of the myths of the founding civilizations—Greek, Roman, Norse, Celtic, Native American, and so on. Make sure too that children have the chance to read new fantasy, in which—let us hope—patterns for the future emerge from the mythic echoes of the past. Yes, we must do these things. But a great proportion of our children will never voluntarily open a book outside the doors of school, mostly because their parents don't. They may never even be able properly to read, but become part of the mind-boggling percentage of functional illiterates which our educational system lets slip through the cracks. You can be pretty sure that when these children were between the ages of two and eleven, they were at the very high end of the scale which in a recent report produced an *average* figure, for children in that age group, of twenty-eight hours a week spent in front of a television set.

Twenty-eight hours a week! Four hours a day, including school-days! That's my idea of hell, not pleasure—proof, if it were needed, that television is a drug.

The screen, small or large, is not intrinsically a bad thing. Like most other drugs, it can serve wonderful ends. The pressure of commerce keeps its standards low, but individuals of talent and determination can use the screen to re-create a mythological pattern as powerful as any story written down, or told aloud. And if one of them does it well, the results can be astounding. *Star Wars* and *E.T.* are both variants of the fantasy hero pattern that I was describing earlier; Luke Skywalker's quest runs through "a galaxy far, far away," and the little Extra-Terrestrial comes from his world to ours and back again. More people have seen those two films, throughout the world, than have seen any other film ever made; not because they are the best films ever made, but because they managed, for a couple of hours, to satisfy the longings of the collective unconscious. "Mum!" said my children, as we left the cinema after seeing *Star Wars* twelve years ago, "it's all about your books!" They sounded indignant, as if they felt George Lucas had been cribbing from *The Dark Is Rising*, but of course he hadn't; their indignation only served to point up the fact that where the archetypes of myth are concerned, there is no such thing as a new story. There is only, as Professor Tolkien observed, the cauldron of story, which is available to all of us through the unconscious, and from which we all draw. Nearly every fantasy author I've ever met has had the experience of having a glorious new idea for a story, only to find that some bard or minstrel had the same idea eight hundred years ago.

Television does not produce fantasy of the quality of *Star Wars*. Nor very often does the cinema, for good and simple reasons. A few years ago I had an idea for what I thought was a fantasy novel, but when I began to work on it I found it wanted to be a film. *The Cloud People*, it was called. So I wrote it as a film treatment. It went to a number of producers from Steven Spielberg on down, and it came back again, and although there's now an

Englishman who has hopes for it, I very much doubt whether it will ever get made, even assuming it's good of its kind. The trouble with my small story is that to become a film it would require a budget of at least thirty million dollars, and at the requisite ration of two-and-a-half to one, it would have to earn at least seventy-five million before it could even break even, let alone make a profit. That's a large risk for a producer to take. I really wish *The Cloud People* had wanted to be a book.

So fantasy and its archetypal patterns are not going to reach a mass audience very often today. Even amongst that limited part of the population which reads books—books, not newspapers or magazines or escapist thrillers or romances—even amongst them, it isn't going to reach everyone. Every teacher or librarian knows the sturdy child who is a dogged realist and thinks fantasy is for the birds. There are more children like that than there are fantasy readers, and from a practical point of view that's probably just as well. Back in the mists of time, as everyone sat around the campfire listening to the shaman telling the sacred stories, there was always the realist in the group. "I don't want to listen to those boring old myths," he said, and he went off on his own and invented the wheel.

"Your books seem to fit me just right," said the little girl. *Those* are the children we have to reach: to drop into the shadowy pool of their unconscious minds a few images that—perhaps, with luck—will echo through their lives and help them understand and even improve their world, our world. If America doesn't have what Aristotle and Mr. Campbell call an ethos, if instead there is a gap, we need to make sure that our children are given an early awareness of the timeless, placeless archetypes of myth. And since we have no one single myth, that has to mean all the different—and yet similar—mythic patterns we inherit, collectively, in this country from our very diverse beginnings. I am speaking not only of ancient myth but of the modern fantasy which is its descendant, its inheritor. Like poetry, these are the books which speak most directly to the imagination. As Ursula

Le Guin once wrote, "It is by such statements as 'Once upon a time there was a dragon,' or 'In a hole in the ground there lived a hobbit'—it is by such beautiful non-facts that we fantastic human beings may arrive, in our peculiar fashion, at the truth."

Parents, teachers, librarians, authors, publishers; we are the people with the responsibility for putting together the right child and the right book. Any child and any book will do, but it helps if they match.

Down I went, in my dream, into the mysterious theater of the unconscious, where all manner of fantastical scenes could be played out—and will be played out, as long as one human mind can respond to another. But high above me, brightly lit, was the place where it all began, full of people lost in their imaginations, reading books. I dreamed about a library, once upon a time.

LONG AGO AND FAR AWAY

A talk for the Children's Literature New England institute,
Travelers in Time, *August 1989*

You look down from the airplane, flying over Britain, and—if you
are lucky, and there is no cloud or fog—you see a patchwork, a
map of the past. It is the story of a people, written upon the land:
a long dialogue between people and place. In one form or
another, men have lived here continuously for more than a million years. They have not molded the country as the glaciers did,
grinding down the peaks and carving out the lakes, but they have
scribbled on the land. And the story can best be read from a long
way away. A long way up. Looking down from a height of three
miles or so, you see their earthworks, their hill forts, their standing stones in mysterious circles and avenues; the pattern of their
farming, both before and after enclosure. You see their old ways
and their modern roads; the spreading tentacles of their villages
and towns. And always, not more than a hundred miles from any
part of these islands, you see the other dominant part of the
place, on whose shifting surface nobody can write. The sea.

If you are English, Scottish, Welsh or Irish—or like most of us,
a mongrel mixture—if you are born and brought up on this long-
occupied land, you acquire by a kind of osmosis a sense of the
continuum of place and time. It's more than a sense of place—

anyone can have that, from a childhood or a chunk of years spent in a particular spot. It's a sort of fluid awareness; a freedom from the shrieking demands of Now, the present moment. Yes, our twentieth-century way of life is geared to the demands of the present, with the television set the ultimate tyrant, tamed only a little by the amber-exuding VCR. But no child is wholly wrapped in the present who has grown up seeing a Norman castle from his or her bedroom window, or walking over the slope of a Neolithic hill fort on the way to school; knowing that a farmer down the road can still plough up bits of a Roman pavement, or a London developer dig up an Elizabethan theater (and then bury it again under a concrete block). Here—now and in England—place implies time. The past is omnipresent, so that small Kay in John Masefield's book *The Midnight Folk* sees a mark on a door which two hundred years earlier had been a plague cross, and knows that the rector found Henry VIII arrowheads when cutting up firewood, and that old Mr. Colway in Naseby dug Civil War bullets out of ancient trees.

This sense of the continuum is a treasure which most of us don't know we possess. Like love, it is most apparent through the size of the aching gap left when it is gone. I had to leave behind my own unthinking awareness of time-place when I went to live in the United States twenty-six years ago, and so ever since then I've come home to Britain at least once a year for a fix, a transfusion; for the reassurance of being, at least for a week or two, plugged in.

In America, it seems to me, the sense of man's long relationship with the land can be found only in the Southwest, in the moonscape country of New Mexico and Arizona where Navajo and Zuni, Pueblo and Hopi respect their soil and hold their rocks sacred. Nowhere else is the time of mankind written so clearly upon the land. New England seems deeply historical to most Americans because men and women have lived there for three hundred years. But those were white men and women, and they threw away time, those first settlers, when they arrived in America and began systematically to destroy the way of life of their American Indian predecessors. Most of them came from Britain, and should have known better. In the previous two thousand years in Britain, during recurring invasions from the Continent, over and over again, in Jung's phrase, the soul of the conquered people had entered that of the conquerors—through the relationship each had had with the same land. In America, the American Indian soul didn't have a chance. The white invaders didn't follow the old pattern of killing the men, raping and breeding with the women, and following the old uses of the land. Instead they killed the men *and* the women, and raped the land. Those of us who live in the United States see the rape still happening, every day. The Roman Englishman put his road from London to Bath, along valleys and around hills in a smooth sweep, using the old tracks but straightening them out when the land allowed, and eight hundred years later it's still there as A40, a graceful piece of the landscape. The English American has carved out I-95 from Florida to Maine, chopping through any bit of land in his way, and he's made a road which is a long ruthless slice, dedicated to the goal of vanishing place and time.

But that's a suicidal goal. Continuity is the only thing that can reconcile our tiny lives to their large surroundings.

Alan Garner wrote about continuity in *The Stone Book Quartet*. The four stories are rooted in one place, Garner's part of Cheshire, which is as crucial to the workings of his imagination as Herefordshire was to Masefield's and Wales is to my own. In that place, in these books, time links the generations through trades that endure: building and making, the carving of stone, the working of iron. A clay pipe lost in one generation is discovered centuries later in another; a loom worked by a father lies unused after his death until his son makes it into a sled for his own grandchild. And deep in the rock is a cave where a bull is painted on a stone wall, in the buried dark, and in each generation the eldest child is taken to look at it. There are many footprints beneath the painting in the dusty ground, from this accumulation of lone brave quests. " 'We've been going a while,' said Father."

That painted bull draws the past into the present, just as the Cheshire dialect of the books draws language through the years like a broom, sweeping away time. Language is organic; it grows and changes and acquires mutations and elisions and shifts of meaning, so that a new edition of the *Oxford English Dictionary* is saluted for keeping us "up with the times." But the old dialects of the English language, and the old languages of Britain, Welsh and the Gaelic, resist erosion more stubbornly. They have the same dogged permanence as the painted bull—or the stone votive axe which is a funnel for human emotion all through time, and always in one place, in Garner's book *Red Shift*.

But *Red Shift* is about more than continuity, and this is not the moment to consider it.

For writers with an inclination to tell stories outside the passage of time, it is easier to interweave the present and the past than to play similarly with the future. The future has its own way of disappearing. In 1963, I published a novel called *Mandrake* which was set in the future (and was therefore labeled, inaccurately, as science fiction). The story was a kind of Armageddon warning about the dire results of damaging our environment. But the future it projected was only seventeen years ahead: it was set in 1980. So today the warning looks pretty silly, because we're still busy damaging our environment, but 1980 has come and gone and Armageddon didn't come with it. The future became the past, when I wasn't looking.

This is a problem we all face every time we look in the mirror. In the case of this book I don't have to solve it, because fortunately *Mandrake* is out of print.

John Masefield plays with the present and the past in those lovely books *The Midnight Folk* and *The Box of Delights*. But he never lets place take him outside time as Alan Garner does. He is a magician; he doesn't care for metaphysics. There's an enchanted passage in *The Midnight Folk* in which the portrait of Kay's great-grandpapa Harker comes alive; he holds out his hand and takes Kay into the painting. As its landscape opens around him, Kay sees the artist in it, painting; and he sees the earlier version of the house in which he now lives and the portrait now hangs. He sees a few other familiar portraits too, painted in earlier years, hanging in unfamiliar places. The past has become the present. But the change is only temporary. Masefield never lets us forget the present; he puts in reminders. Like this one: "A black cat, with white throat and paws, which had been ashes for forty years, rubbed up against Great-grandpapa Harker's legs, and then, springing on the arm of his chair, watched the long dead sparrows in the plum tree which had been firewood a quarter of a century ago."

Masefield's books may seem to be time-haunted, but the true center of their haunting is magic. The old man Cole Hawlings appears to Kay in *The Box of Delights*, with his little dog and his magic box which will move you fast or slow, make you small or large, or take you back into the past or forward again to the present. "I do date from pagan times," he says, and he foretells the future, and disappears, sometimes, into the past. He is, however, a linear fellow. He turns out to be one Ramon Lully who a long time ago invented an elixir to keep him alive in the future, and wanted to do a swap with Master Arnold of Todi who'd invented a box to take him back into the past. Ramon/Cole ends up with the box after Master Arnold goes too far back into the past and gets lost there. Through Time to the present he carries the haunting warning that *The Wolves Are Running*, and its echoes linger in the air even after the wolf villains get their comeuppance.

But then Masefield cops out, in an extraordinary narrative aberration, and announces that the whole book has been nothing but Kay's dream. This is the act of a man so firmly rooted in Time, and the realities of life and death, that after bringing an illusion brilliantly to life he chooses to kill it stone dead. "Only a dream!" I remember being outraged when I first read—or more accurately, heard—the end of *The Box of Delights;* the only unreal part of the book, I thought, was the last page, on which Kay woke up, and Masefield tried to pretend that the Box of Delights had never existed at all.

John Masefield put his toe outside Time, and then went back into it. (I must ask the reader's indulgence for the arbitrary way in which the word "time" is sometimes capitalized and sometimes not, in this talk; there are occasions, generally when I'm speaking of it as an abstract concept, when I simply feel it *needs* a capital letter.) When I was a young writer I stayed in the mainstream of linear time too: *Over Sea, Under Stone* is a relatively uncomplicated adventure story about the pursuit in the present of an object hidden in the past. Nobody leaves the present moment. My three unremarkable and singularly dated children, by Arthur Ransome out of E. Nesbit, find a manuscript containing a map which records the hiding, centuries before, of a chalice, a grail, which is called "the last trust of the old world" hidden "until the day comes."

"The darkness draws toward Cornwall," says the writer of the old manuscript, "and the long ships creep to our shore," and he must hide the grail.

So therefore I trust it to this land, over sea and under stone, and I mark here the signs by which the proper man in the proper place may know where it lies, the signs that wax and wane but do not die. The secret of its charge I may not write, but carry unspoken to my grave. Yet the man who finds the grail and has other words from me will know, by both, the secret for himself. And for him is the charge, the promise and the proof, and in his day the Pendragon shall come again. And that day shall see a new Logres, with evil cast out; when the old world shall appear no more than a dream.

(*Appear* no more than a dream. Not *be* no more than a dream.) The story which comes out of all this is quite simple, in terms of time. There's even an image in the book expressing its shape, without intending to:

"Straight as an arrow the long white road of the moon's reflection stretched toward them across the surface of the sea, like a path from the past and a path to the future. . . ."

Everyone in this room has done a great deal of reading for this institute on "Travelers in Time," and I dare say a lot of the piles of books had Eliot's *Four Quartets* at one end and Stephen Hawking's *A Brief History of Time* at the other. My pile also had to include my own five-book sequence *The Dark Is Rising*, and I read these five, continuously and in order, for the first time since I published the last of them twelve years ago. This was a very odd sensation. For the first time I saw what I had been doing. I suppose I was in fact discovering what my unconscious had done. This is something every author knows about. Very often, in all the arts, the thing we make is not necessarily the thing we thought we were making—and I don't just mean the occasional disaster, or the everlasting disappointing gap between the idea and its realization. The mind produces its conscious intention—and then the imagination takes over. In *The Dark Is Rising* I thought I'd been telling five stories linked into one, as the movements of a symphony blend into a whole. I hadn't noticed that in the last four of the five books I had at the same time been trying all the while, over and over, to write a definition of Time.

The first book of the *Dark Is Rising* sequence, *Over Sea, Under Stone*, deals with linear time—like *The Midnight Folk* and *The Box of Delights*, though in a much less luminous and magical fashion. These books follow what Stephen Hawking calls the psychological arrow of time: "the direction," he says, "in which we *feel* time passes, the direction in which we remember the past but not the future." The same is true of Alan Garner's early books, *The Weirdstone of Brisingamen* and *The Moon of Gomrath*. They tell magical stories, growing out of Alderley Edge in Cheshire, and they run between "the long ago of the world" and the present. There's one moment of breakthrough in the Eve of Gomrath, "one of the four nights of the year when Time and

Forever mingle." But really these books are not concerned with time, but with what Garner calls, in a lovely phrase, "the world of magic, that lies as near and unknown to us as the back of a shadow."

Then sometime in the 1960s, neither of us knowing the other's work, Alan Garner and I both moved in the same direction as writers and began playing with Time. Or maybe Time began playing with us. We are very different authors, but we started to express the same preoccupation. At least so it seems to me now, looking back. Alan wrote *The Owl Service* and I wrote the second of my sequence of books, *The Dark Is Rising*. Until this point I hadn't actually known there was going to be a sequence. In that book, Will Stanton walks out of his sleeping present-day house into the snow-covered countryside of a time centuries earlier—and finds that people are expecting him. This happens on page 195 of a 780-page sequence of novels, and it's the moment when the author too walks out of a door, of sorts, from real time to—something else.

There's a lot of walking through doors in *The Dark Is Rising*. Doors are almost as important to the book as snowfalls and rainstorms and claps of thunder. I didn't multiply them on purpose; I think the image simply took over, because my imagination was so intent on leaving the world it had inhabited before and going through into another kind of preoccupation, another world. Will Stanton finds himself on a hillside facing two immense carved wooden doors, standing closed, alone, surreal; and when he pushes them open, "the light and the day and the world changed, so that he forgot utterly what they had been." The doors, his master Merriman tells him later, are for the Old Ones of the universe "our great gateway into Time"—which is to say, out of Time as we, you and I, know it.

"We of the Circle are planted only loosely within Time," says Merriman. "The doors are a way through it, in any direction we may choose. For all times coexist, and the future can sometimes affect the past, even though the past is a road that leads to the future. . . . But men cannot understand this."

No. Men can't—except Mr. Eliot. I couldn't. But I went on trying to, as I wrote. "It is a mystery," says Hawkin, in *The Dark Is
Rising*, to Will. "The Old Ones can travel in time as they choose.
You are not bound by the laws of the universe as we know them."
So, an Old One brings Hawkin forward in time from his own
thirteenth century to the nineteenth century, and in the nineteenth he betrays the Light and is sent back to the thirteenth to
become the Walker, doomed to carry one of the great Signs until
Will, who had watched his betrayal in the nineteenth century, is
born into the twentieth century to take over this six-hundred-
year-old burden . . .

If you can stand the whirling of the roundabout, this complex-
ity takes you to a stillness that is outside any fixed concept of
Time—and also outside religion. In *The Dark Is Rising*, the force
of the Dark attacks a group of the Old Ones while they are in a
church, and is driven back by the Signs, each of which is a cross
within a circle. The rector of the church says: well, of course. A
cross. One of the Old Ones points out that these crosses were
made long before Christianity, long before Christ. The rector
says, "But not before God."

Will says, "There's not really any before or after, is there?
Everything that matters is outside Time, and comes from there
and can go there."

"You mean infinity," says the rector.

" 'Not altogether,' said the Old One that was Will. 'I mean the
part of all of us, and of all the things we think and believe, that
has nothing to do with yesterday, or today or tomorrow, because
it belongs at a different kind of level. Yesterday is still there, on
that level. Tomorrow is there too. You can visit either of them.
And all Gods are there, and all the things they have ever stood
for. And,' he added sadly, 'the opposite too.' "

"Outside Time." These books speak of outside and inside as if
there were two parts to Time. In *Greenwitch* Merriman says of a
creature of the Dark, destroyed by his own ambition, "The Wild
Magic has taken him to outer Time, from which he may never
properly come back." In *The Dark Is Rising*, Will hears Merriman

80

speak into his mind "from somewhere outside Time." In the final book, *Silver on the Tree*, if Will does not reclaim the six Signs, "the High Magic which guards them will take them outside Time." There is always this double image: the moving river which is linear time, the time in which human beings are conscious of living, and the infinite plain which it crosses, from any point of which any point of the moving river can be reached. Or not reached, if some prohibition stands in the way.

This plain is the continuum of place/time. The image is imperfect, but then images usually are. Like most writers, I make a picture to communicate anything I can't properly explain; and the pictures are not only never perfect, they're never original either. And in the long run, in this cosmology, there aren't even any pictures. Merriman says in *Silver on the Tree* that eventually all those of the Light will go out of Time: "as I shall go before long, and as one day long hence Will will go too." And at the climax of the confrontation between Dark and Light, the Lords of the Dark "fall backwards out of Time, and disappear."

No image, no picture. Just—out. Into mystery.

Partway into my notes on rereading *Silver on the Tree*, I wrote, "It makes me giddy, the way this book flickers in and out of Time, interweaving past and present and future." That flickering seems to be an essential part of my fantasy novels; they interweave time in story. I can't however do that in the abstract, and nor I think can Alan Garner; we have to do it through place.

My places are a piece of the Thames Valley and the Chiltern Hills, a piece of Southern Cornwall, and more than either a piece of mid-Wales, around Cader Idris, on the southern edge of Snowdonia. (I was there last week, and part of me is always there.) In that magnificent book *The Owl Service*, Alan Garner switches from his native Cheshire to a different valley in Wales which becomes a whirlpool of time: a container for the power of the story from the Mabinogion of Lleu, Blodeuwedd and Gronw Pebyr, which happened once in myth and here, in this valley and this book, is always happening.

You could say, I suppose, that *The Owl Service* is the story, on a most extraordinary scale, of the laying of a ghost. But what is a ghost but an echo of time, in place? Someone in the book suggests to Gwyn that the myth haunts the valley.

"Not haunted," said Gwyn after a while. "More like—still happening."

And later on, Roger says in exasperation, "You'd think it was the only thing that's ever happened in the valley!"

"That is right," says Huw.

And then later on again: "I don't know where I am," says Alison. "Yesterday, today, tomorrow—they don't mean anything. I feel they're here at the same time, waiting."

Yesterday, today and tomorrow, waiting. Their focus is Huw Halfbacon, unchanging as the stone by the river; magician and laborer, ancient and enduring, waiting like a salmon in this pool of time. I use the image of a pool for Alan's book and I find I used it once in *Silver on the Tree*, too. "We will strive at our separate tasks across the centuries," says Merriman there to Will, "through the waves of time, touching and parting, parting and touching in the pool that whirls forever."

And the pool always means a particular part of what Merriman calls "this long-worked land so many centuries on the anvil." In *The Owl Service* it's as if the valley is a magnet for all parts of time. "My Mom hates the place," says Gwyn, "but she can't get rid of it, see?"

We all have places we can't get rid of, loved or hated; places which bring the past into the present. When I was little, walking to school through the Buckinghamshire countryside which is the setting for *The Dark Is Rising*, we used to pass the top of a dark, wooded little track which was known locally as Tramps Alley. The name was accurate; once in a while it was refuge for shambling old wanderers with five tattered overcoats, newspaper in their shoes and trousers held up with string. We were strictly warned to keep clear of them.

I sent Will down Tramps Alley in *The Dark Is Rising*, and he did indeed encounter a tramp—the Walker—and after that a number of traumatic events which almost cost him one of the great Signs. His master Merriman told him severely that he had been saved from disaster only by the fact that this little lane happened to be one of the ancient routes of the Light: an Old Way. And my pen stopped still, writing that, because I suddenly remembered the proper name of Tramps Alley. "Don't call it that," our parents used to say fastidiously. "You know its real name is Oldway Lane."

Thirty years later, long after my family had moved to Wales and long after I'd gone to live in America, I was driving once from London to Wales when I found I'd missed the turning from the M4 that would take me to the A40, my road home. I turned north at random, and pulled into a side road to check where I was on the map. And I found I was right on top of the once green countryside of *The Dark Is Rising*, covered largely now by stretches of concrete and macadam, and when I looked up at the street sign of the little road where I'd stopped, lined with tidy houses, it said, "Oldway Lane."

Place and time. Time and place. For the aborigines of Australia, the Ancestors dreamed place into existence, and to learn about place is to remember that dreaming, calling back time. The boundaries of things blur. Place seems so definite when you look around this room, time so precise when you look at your watch; but look more closely and those boundaries blur too. If you look as closely as a theoretical physicist, you can end up with Stephen Hawking's proposal (in *A Brief History of Time*) of a universe having no boundary or edge, no beginning or end: infinite space, infinite time. It's not too different from the endless plain of time in the *Dark Is Rising* books, the haunted recurrence of *The Owl Service*, the passion reverberating through the centuries in *Red Shift*.

Alan Garner's *Red Shift* is a brilliant, dense book and I would not presume to try to unravel its evocation of Time. I am a writer, not a critic or teacher, and I have enough trouble unraveling my own. But it seems to me that this novel is more profoundly concerned with the continuum of place and time than any other I have ever read. It doesn't talk about time; everything is in the patterning of the story. We flicker in and out of Roman time, Civil War time, present time; the future stretches before the first of these; the past lies behind the third; the second has both past and future, it echoes to and fro. Within Garner's piece of Cheshire, all three coexist, and fierce emotion runs through the continuum, erupting in violent death or in the violence of loving.

The thunderbolt, the votive axe through which Macey is possessed, Macey who was seven when the Romans came, will be found by Civil War Thomas and built by Thomas and Madge into the chimney of the house in whose ruin present-day Tom and Jan will find it. Sounds and events echo backwards. Orion hangs over them all, turning. And the galaxies retreat through the red end of the spectrum: "the further they go, the faster they leave. The sky's emptying."

So is the ferocity of emotion. "Pip loves Brian," says the first line of the graffiti Tom and Jan find on a wall. Then underneath it there's another line: "not really now not any more."

"Everywhere's been good or bad for somebody at some time," says Jan, "so there's no point in moping about Pip and bloody Brian, whoever they were."

Not really now not any more.

Alan Garner said once, at one of these institutes, "We have to tell stories, to unriddle the world." None of us is going to unriddle time, but we shall go on trying. None of us, not even Stephen Hawking, is going to resolve definitively the question of the real relationship between space and time, the real origin and fate of the universe. "*Real* is a hard word," says my minstrel, Gwion, in *Silver on the Tree*. "Almost as hard as *true*, or *now.*"

He says something else too that is not unrelated to the theme of *Red Shift*, though without its passionate bitterness. "For ever and ever, we say when we are young, and in our prayers. Twice, we say it. For ever and ever . . . so that a thing may be for ever, a life or a love or a quest, and yet begin again, and be for ever just as before. And any ending that may seem to come is not truly an ending, but an illusion. For time does not die, Time has neither beginning nor end, and so nothing can end or die that has once had a place in Time."

> And the end and the beginning were always there,
> (said Mr. Eliot)
> Before the beginning and after the end,
> And all is always now.

Now and in England. In *The Dark Is Rising,* in England, the moment of the opening of the Old Ones' doors through Time is marked always for Will Stanton by the sound of a delicate, elusive music: "a sweet beckoning sound that was the space between waking and dreaming, yesterday and tomorrow, memory and imagining." Music was the only image I could find for the demonstration of a mystery. It still is. Music is after all made of time, and carries it down the centuries in a chain of renewal—like the seasons, and the turning year, and all other patterns of life, death, new life. Music is an echo, like all life, spreading out over the continuum like the widening ripples in a pool. When Jack Langstaff draws you into a music at the end of this institute, and you sing, think of the echo, that carries our mystery from the blue end of the spectrum to the red, all through the rainbow of time, out beyond the universe.

The psychologist Diane Paolitto has reminded us that in the early years, for all children, "calendar time still lies somewhere in the past, enshrouded in mystery." To be reconciled to the nature of Time, perhaps we need to rediscover that early, unprecise perception. When we are children, we have a tranquil acceptance of mystery which is driven out of us later on, by curiosity and education and experience. But it is possible to find one's way back. With affection and respect, I disagree totally with Penelope Lively's conviction about the "absolute impossibility of recovering a child's vision." There *are* ways, imperfect, partial, fleeting, of looking again at a mystery through the eyes we used to have. Children are not different animals. They are us, not yet wearing our heavy jacket of time.

There's one other image in *The Dark Is Rising* that I would toss into the pool. I put it into the novel, as I did so many others, without really knowing then what I was about. The Book of Gramarye (the old word for magic and mystery), the book which has in it all the wisdom of the world and of the Old Ones, lies waiting for Will Stanton. Where? Of all places: inside a clock. Its protection is the swing of the pendulum, the passing of time. And when Will has learned its contents, when Gramarye has been released into the world, that pendulum which is Time destroys the book, in "a soundless explosion, a blinding flash of dark light, a great roar of energy that could not be seen or heard."

One day, that's what Time will do to the earth. But the galaxy will rush on, across the plain, across the pool. Traveling. Gramarye, the mystery, will keep it going.

Moving On

A talk for the Children's Literature New England institute,
Homecoming, August 1990

Here is a quotation from John Ruskin, slightly condensed: from his little collection of lectures published as *Sesame and Lilies* in 1864. It's the beginning of a small story I want to tell you.

> Home is the place of peace; the shelter not only from all injury but from all terror, doubt and division. In so far as it is not this, it is not home; so far as the anxieties of the outer life penetrate into it, it ceases to be home; it is then only a part of that outer world which you have roofed over, and lighted fire in. But so far as it is a sacred place, a temple of the hearth watched over by Household Gods, before whose faces none may come but those whom they can receive with love—so far it vindicates the name, and fulfils the praise, of Home.

When I was a child, that piece of prose hung on the wall in the front hall of our little semidetached house in Buckinghamshire, twenty miles outside London. It was written in elaborate Olde Englyshe script, and set behind glass in a narrow black frame, and I didn't pay it much attention. Words on a wall struck me as rather boring, and so did John Ruskin, and I never even read this little framed homily all the way through.

Never, until the year when I was ten years old and my father had what was known then as a nervous breakdown. The pressures of his personal life joined up with the delayed effect of the things he'd seen very recently during World War II, and long ago during World War I, and they all exploded in his mind so that one night he didn't come home. Instead of catching the commuter train from London as usual, he took the family savings out of a bank account, perhaps intending to run away; then he traveled across London to visit his mother's grave, perhaps looking vainly for the person who could make everything better. Then he walked two miles to Westminster Bridge, where he stood for a long time trying to make himself jump into the River Thames.

But he didn't, couldn't, jump. He went home, late at night, to the little Buckinghamshire house with no telephone, where my mother was by now frantic, and my little brother and I sitting up late with her, terrified, waiting. When the door opened, he said, "I only came back because of the children," and he burst into tears. He then spent the next three months lying in bed with his face turned to the wall, a classic undiagnosed untreated case of depression, and we had to tiptoe around the house wondering why Daddy didn't want to see us any more.

One day, years later, he stood me in front of that framed Ruskin quote on the wall—"Home is the place of peace; the shelter from all injury . . ."—and he read it all aloud to me. *"Never forget that,"* he said.

So I never did. From the days when we were very small, the war had already made home a place of practical sanctuary, with its womblike little caves into which we were thrust when the bombs fell: the air-raid shelter under the back lawn, or in emergency the cupboard under the stairs. Twenty years later I put the whole picture, intact, into an autobiographical novel called *Dawn of Fear*: my peaceful home, an island refuge in a world of distress and threat.

I happened to be an abnormally shy child, so home also took on abnormally large importance as a place of emotional security and refuge. Several times in my life, at some really major emotional crisis, I've heard myself say in my head—or even aloud—"I want to go home." And the childhood home was the one I meant. Origin and sanctuary in one. When I was that introverted child, my favorite chapter in *Wind in the Willows* was of course "Dulce Domum," and my favorite character was Mole. I didn't just identify with Mole; I *was* Mole. So was my younger brother. At nine years old he was even typecast as Mole in the school play.

I knew, when I was a child, that home wasn't just a geographical place. My mother showed us that by announcing from time to time, "Tomorrow I'm going to take you home," and carrying us off on a two-hour bus journey to her parents' house. She'd never lived there; they had moved to it long after her marriage. But for her it was home nonetheless: family, people, *her* people. This always distressed me a little—*we* were her family and home, weren't we?—and thirty years later I daresay I distressed my own children by doing exactly the same thing. But it taught them, as it taught me, that alongside the first home there will come another, and another: that we each have the home of origin, always remembered, always (if you're lucky) forgiving and welcoming; and we also have after that the home of the present, the current refuge or family.

Parents feel their own *frisson* the first time children are heard to perform this doubling of vision; I remember my son—at home—talking about going home to his fraternity; my daughter Kate doing the same about her off-campus apartment. Earlier this year I heard her doing it again, in a train rocking through Russia, where I was visiting her. "I'll write after I get home," she said, and this time she meant a family with whom she was living for a year in Lvov, in the Ukraine. Like roving limpets we all attach ourselves to a sequence of places, and circumstance, like the sea, washes us from rock to rock. Eventually, another train carried Kate from the Ukraine to begin the journey back to the first home—just as in my book *Silver on the Tree,* in the *Dark Is Rising* sequence, a train rushes through Time carrying its passengers from the present into the past. Perhaps I have a peculiar obsession with long-distance trains, but they seem to me to provide more of a metaphor for life than any other form of transport. Maybe it's those rails, which have a firm place in our imagery: if you stay on the rails, you're okay, if you go off the rails, you're wacko.

I remember one other train, periodical but particular, from the days when I was a young reporter, working on a Sunday newspaper in London. Sometimes, then, I would leave the office at midnight on Saturday and go straight to catch the night train to North Wales, my second home, where my parents lived their last twenty years. In my swaying bunk I'd wake up at about four A.M. to see the mountains rising all around, and the land grew more and more beautiful as the train rocked me back to my family, with its echoes of my childhood, until at last I could see the long limitless horizon of the sea. The sea, first home of all life on earth; you can hardly get closer to your origin than that.

But when after those weekends I went back to London, from sea and family and mountains, I was going home too. Not just to my own place but to my own occupation, my professional tribe. The community of work offers another very particular homecoming embrace; if you love what you do, there's a welcoming quality about the workplace, whether it's office, school, college, library, ship, factory, theater, coal mine—or the city room of a newspaper.

The same goes of course for larger communities: village, town, city, province, state, nation. The biggest mistake Adolf Hitler made during World War II was to try to invade Britain in 1940; all he achieved was to give fifty million people a passionate determination to keep him away from their home. Winston Churchill's rolling phrases spoke for the whole nation: "We shall defend our island, whatever the cost may be, we shall fight on the beaches, we shall fight on the landing grounds, we shall fight in the fields and in the streets, we shall fight in the hills. We shall never surrender." And when the British Army suffered defeat in France and 350,000 men were beaten back to the beaches of Dunkirk, almost every amateur sailor in the south of England put out across the English Channel in an amazing polyglot fleet of little boats, "to bring our boys home." A sense of belonging is a very potent animal instinct: we're all territorial, we all cling to our flock or herd or tribe.

When I was twenty-six years old, I took the peculiar risk of going against this instinct. I left every aspect of home: place, family, friends, occupation, nation—the lot, and I married an American and came to live in the U.S.A. If put back in the same situation, I should probably do the same again, but I wouldn't say it was a reasoned choice. When you are uprooted in this way, and leave home completely and suddenly, what you leave is not a place only, but the whole fabric of life. You leave the sights and sounds and smells of your native environment, familiar and reassuring; the particular patterns of day and night, climate and weather, roads and rivers, and above all, people, all the different layers of relationships. You lose things you had never realized you possessed: a way of thinking, an ingrained pattern of assumptions and prejudices, and of delights felt never so acutely as when they are no longer there. Of course you gain things too, but they don't fill these particular holes, because they are a different shape.

The loss of all these is the fate of any emigrant. He—and she—try to carry with them, like lifebelts, some aspects of the old home, and that's what accounts for the fact that this melting pot called the United States contains so many lumps. A home in Minneapolis or Chicago, or almost any American city, may be totally American, and yet it will cling by family tradition to the language and cultural patterns of some other country that perhaps no living member of the family has even seen.

And in the refugee, the longings of the emigrant are doubled. It is our nature to cling to home, and to mourn its loss. Today, we can look back at the 1930s and feel astounded that in that dangerous time so many German Jews declined to leave Germany, in spite of the growth of the Nazi movement and all the doom-laden hints of the impending Holocaust. But those people who didn't leave were not only Jewish, they were German, and their deepest instinct was to stay at home. It's another version of the same instinct which throbs so perilously through the Middle East now: the Israelis fiercely guard the first home they have had for two thousand years, the Palestinians fiercely strive to get their own home back.

Estrangement, dispossession, is of course something the Jews have always known about. It permeates their literature, their liturgy, their whole consciousness. Related to it is that sudden, total dispossession called banishment. It has no formal place in the world today; the only people who feel themselves banished from a country these days tend to be voluntary criminal exiles who are keeping away because they'd be arrested if they came back in. But in the England of Richard II, banishment was a fate to be dreaded only just behind death or mutilation. Shakespeare, that total Englishman, has the Earl of Mowbray, banished by Richard, reacting as if his world had come to an end.

Then thus I turn me from my country's light,
To dwell in solemn shades of endless night.

Estrangement. Feeling oneself a stranger. It's the clear opposite of being at home. It's Ruth, full of good intentions about following Naomi wherever she may go, but finding herself in the end "sick for home, standing in tears amid the alien corn." To some degree, it describes a great many people in this country who are obliged by the law to carry with them at all times the green card, symbol of the resident alien. (The government actually started coloring them blue a few years ago, but they're still known as green cards.) If you come upon a green-card holder who has lived in the United States for more than ten years without becoming an American citizen, it's a fair bet that he or she is still, somewhere deep down, homesick.

I can tell you a lot about homesickness; I am an expert on the matter of living and loving across a divide, on the kind of ache that is bearable only because its absence would signify emptiness, the loss of all feeling. The Welsh call this ache *hiraeth*, and by that word they mean something more than homesickness: they mean a kind of deep longing of the soul. They guard the value of the word, and are contemptuous of those who use it lightly. Every year at the Royal Albert Hall in London there is a rally of the London Welsh Society, and plump successful Welsh emigrés from England or America get up on their feet and sing the national anthem "Land of My Fathers," and they weep. And back in Wales the real Welshmen mock them, and wonder aloud why, if they're so homesick, these sentimentalists don't give up their nice fat foreign incomes and come home.

But for some of us there are other, stronger reasons why you can't go home, not to live, and so there is this deep longing inside you that will never go away, until you die, and perhaps not even then if you are buried in the wrong place. My *Dark Is Rising* books were written out of *hiraeth*, the longing; it infuses every image and description in them. Like many authors published for children, I've said often that I don't write *for* children, but for myself, and in the case of these books it's especially true. It's true, that is, of the last four of the five books of the sequence, which were written after I'd lived for more than ten years in the United States. These four are quite different from the first book, *Over Sea, Under Stone*, which was written when I still lived in London. (For one thing, they're better books, and I should hope so too after ten years of practice. The worst thing you can ever say to an author is, "Oh, my favorite of all your books is the first"—it's like telling him that his whole life has been a long downhill slide. Which is something that in black moments he often suspects anyway.) Those last four *Dark Is Rising* books are layered with Englishness and Welshness, the two sides of my mongrel British nature; they're full of the history and geography of the British Isles, their time and place, their people and weather and skies and spells, all echoing to and fro. I couldn't live there in reality, so I lived there in my books. Perhaps the sequence put the *hiraeth* to rest, in its most painful and acute form, because I seem not to have written anything about Britain since, except for three small retellings of folktales.

Everyone leaves the first home. Time passes, nothing stays the same. We all leave childhood behind, even though that process may take decades, and not really be completed until our parents die. It's not an easy process; perhaps there's no such thing as easy growth, unless you're a dandelion. It isn't easy because you have to fight all the way against the pull of home. Not all the aspects of that word are warm and cozy; there are many that are sinister. There's home as octopus, home as snare; home as Venus flytrap, home as black hole. Home can be the place you can't escape from, or haven't the courage to leave or replace; the womb you have never really left. This is the dark side of home, and we should not lose sight of it, in a romantic haze of nostalgia. If one is to grow, home has to be replaced, over and over again, in a progression through life.

If the progression is a good one, its beginnings disappear into a mist, reappearing sometimes when we least expect them. I have a dear friend called Zoë Dominic, born and bred in London, who is a photographer. She just turned seventy. One day last year she was photographing the English composer Carl Davis, and he asked if he could have some prints sent to his home address.

"Of course," said Zoë, and she took out a pen and waited to hear where he lived.

"Thirty-four—" Carl Davis said, and then he paused. "Oh God," he said, "my brain's going. I can't remember my own address."

"Ambleside Avenue," Zoë said.

He stared at her. "How did you know?" he said.

This time Zoë was staring at him. "You don't mean you actually live there?"

"That's right," Carl said. "Thirty-four Ambleside Avenue, Streatham."

Zoë said, "That's the house where I was born."

Carl looked at her face and he said, "I think you'd better come to lunch."

So back she went to the house where she had been born, where she'd lived until she was nine, and she looked at it again for the first time in sixty years. It seemed smaller, of course; they always do. The ground floor seemed unrecognizable, having had walls knocked down to make an open-plan modern space; but Zoë put her hand on the newel post of the staircase and heard herself cry, "Oh! You've kept the knob!" And she was back as a little girl again, hurtling down the stairs with her brother and swinging round at the bottom, hanging on to that knob.

Then she remembered her night nursery. Hers had been the kind of family that had a day nursery and a night nursery and a nanny. The Davises took her up to the top of the house and showed her the room, but now it was Carl's sound studio, and jammed with all kinds of high-tech audio equipment. Zoë looked at it blankly. She said, full of nostalgia, "There used to be an old-fashioned gas fire in here, when I was a child."

"Oh yes!" they cried. "We put it in the garage!" And they all went out to the garage and cleared a pile of junk, and Zoë, this sophisticated theater photographer, found herself facing the fire beside which she had sat with Nanny, drinking her bedtime milk every night, after her bath.

"It was very odd indeed," she said to me later. "It was like walking into a totally strange landscape, and finding in it clues to something buried very deep inside yourself."

In memory, the first home doesn't change. In real life it certainly does; most of the green fields of my *Dark Is Rising* countryside are covered in concrete now. But so long as we progress, this doesn't matter. The memory goes with us.

And in each new place or condition, we make ourselves at home. That's the progression, on and on. We very rarely die when transplanted; there's always something to nourish us, to catch at the roots. For me, transplanted, it was my children. "I only came back because of the children," said my father, out of his deep despair, and I know what he meant. I go on living in America as a resident alien primarily because my children are wholly American and this is *their* home. We make such choices all the time, between old ground and new. It's like that laudable but incomplete sentiment that Victorian ladies used to embroider on pillows: "Home is where the heart is." Home means people. Sometimes one person. That's our choice.

There have always been some who don't have this choice. We have a new label for them today. A generation ago, the destitute man with nowhere to go, with his worldly belongings in a brown paper parcel, would have been called a tramp, or a bum, or a hobo. Today he's "one of the homeless," and he or she is very likely instead to be none of those three things. Instead he's a victim, of a culture in which home is not something you find or are given, but something you have to buy. Homeless, helpless, hopeless: the words summon one another up. We recognize today that the homeless person has a dire, basic problem, though as a society we certainly don't do enough about it. He, she, needs to belong—somewhere, anywhere. To be attached. Even the most helplessly destitute try to attach themselves to *something*: to a space under a railway bridge, a handcart full of junk, a particular doorway on a New York City sidewalk—if the passing cop will turn a blind eye.

It's possible to be without that sense of attachment even if, unlike the homeless, you do happen to have a geographical spot in which to live. Back in England, when I worked for *The Sunday Times* and had graduated from reporter to feature writer, my editor gave me the job of writing a major series of articles on Loneliness. This was a subject which defied most formal methods of research, so I was allowed to put a tiny three-line advertisement in my newspaper's section of Classified Advertisements, known as the small-ads. It said something like: "Writer studying loneliness would be grateful for any opinions or information," and it gave no name, just a box number.

The next week, the small-ad department was staggered by the amount of mail that came in to this box number. There were mailbags full of letters, and some of the letters were very fat and long. I had hundreds and hundreds of them, so many that in the end we had to send out a circularized note of thanks as their only reply. For twenty-five years I've been haunted by feelings of guilt about these unanswered correspondents, because of course each of them was lonely, suffering from a feeling of estrangement from other people or simply from life. And each one of them was responding, with hope and often an outpouring of emotion, to this unknown person who had said to them, "Talk to me."

"For heaven's sake," said my editor. "Are you going to be pen pal to several hundred people—or nanny, or psychiatrist? Let them read your articles. You don't have to hold their hands." And I suppose he was right, though I can't think the articles helped anyone much, because all they did was to describe the extraordinary extent of loneliness in British society, and urge everyone to remember that no man is an island and that we should all love our neighbors more. All those people, feeling cut off, detached, estranged—most of them had houses, but I'm not sure they had homes. Is there as high a proportion of lonely people in the United States? Do Americans feel more connected one with another? I suppose I could find out by putting a "small-ad" in *The New York Times*, but I don't think I'm going to take the risk.

In the last novel I wrote, called *Seaward*, a boy and a girl leave their homes: not voluntarily, but because circumstance forces them out. Each goes on a journey, as we all do, and the connection that they find is with each other. It's also, I suppose, the only new home they find. I've talked about life being a succession of homecomings, to a new place or condition each time, but it seems to me that I don't write stories which ever lead to home. They start there, but after that beginning point they are all journeys. And the successive homecomings are generally relationships, found on the open road. Cally and Westerly, the girl and boy in *Seaward*, are offered a home at the end of their story—by Life and Death, who are as closely interlinked as brother and

Thou goest home this night to thy perpetual home,
To thine eternal bed, to thine eternal slumber.
The sleep of the seven lights be thine, beloved,
The sleep of the seven joys be thine, beloved,
The sleep of the seven slumbers be thine, beloved,
On the arm of Jesus of Blessings, the Christ of Grace.

It seems to me that only the last line of this lament is
Christian. The rest is about a homecoming that is older than
Christianity, older than religion. Earth to earth, dust to dust,
ashes to ashes is about as basic a directive as you can get: by our
physical nature we are bound to the cycle of birth and death,
birth and death, over and over. Birth, death and rebirth, of
course—but the rebirth is a different new life, here on earth, not
the revival of an old one.

Here on earth. This is where the cycle happens, this is where
we live. This is the ultimate concept of home, this particular
almost-sphere spinning through space and time. We don't take
care of it very well, considering that if we foul this nest we shall
never have another one. Like most living authors I don't believe
in writing books for children with a deliberate Message, but if I
were ever to become a missionary that's what I would preach.
Home is this planet, and the people who live on it. Take care of
it, and of them.

My daughter Kate brought back from the Soviet Union an
environmental poster which some of you may have seen: a great
blue sweep of sky, of space, and floating in it a small round
image of Earth, that beautiful dappled view of it that only astro-
nauts see. The legend on the poster is very short: it says, in
Russian, *"Nyet droogovo doma."* "There is no other home."

Earth. That's our home. *Nash dom,* in Russian. And as I wrote
that down, drafting this talk, I suddenly remembered the quiet
green road called Huntercombe Lane which I used as the back-
bone of my book *The Dark Is Rising.* It was a Buckinghamshire
road where I used to walk and bicycle as a child, very near my

99

childhood home, my home of origin. It was the road I summoned up out of homesickness, as I sat writing the book in a foreign country, and I put my hero Will Stanton into all the familiar places along the road: the manor house, the Church of St. James the Less, a farm, a wood full of cawing rooks—even the local vicarage (though I tossed the vicar out, and put in Will's family instead).

There was one other landmark on that road, which has no place in the story of *The Dark Is Rising* except perhaps for a fleeting reference somewhere. It was an abbey, set back behind a crumbling brick wall. There were monks inside, though we never saw them; it was a very reticent order, Trappists, perhaps. And the place was called, I remember now for the first time in decades, Nashdom Abbey. Nashdom: Nash Dom. "Our home." Perhaps it was founded by a bunch of homesick Russians, a long time ago. And perhaps I have forgotten them all this time because they tried to do something I never have: to make one other home, after the first, and stay in it always.

So far as I know, the community is still there. Moles, all of them, living in their rediscovered Mole End; it's an image I would have loved when I was a child. But now, in spite of homesickness and *hiraeth*, I don't think I envy them. As writer and as individual, I left the first home, taking a backpack of memories with me as nourishment, and went on around this earth, nash dom. Traveling, I found all the other homes thereafter in people, rather than places. And perhaps in the dreams and fantasies inside my own head.

Come to think of it, I began life as Mole, and I seem to have ended as the Water Rat.

WORLDS APART

A talk for the Children's Literature New England institute, Worlds Apart, Oxford, England, August 1992

Jack Langstaff and I went for a walk up St. Giles yesterday, and I took him inside Somerville College and into the main quadrangle, and I said proudly, "That was my room—that one up there." Jack and I are old friends, so he made the right admiring noises—luckily he had his back to the chapel, which is one of the ugliest buildings in the University of Oxford. And as we went out again I breathed a great sigh of relief, because I'd laid the ghost of an incident which I must now confess to you.

Fifteen years or so ago, I'd been driving my two American children on our annual trip from London Airport to North Wales to see their grandparents, and I thought that for once we would not bypass Oxford but drive through it, so they could see where Mummie went to university. I hadn't clapped eyes on Oxford for more than a decade, but I found St. Giles, and as I drove up it into the Woodstock Road I cried with great emotion and confidence, "Look! That big building on the left! That's Mummie's college!"

And as I drove on, damp-eyed, my six-year-old daughter Kate said, "Mummie, there was a big notice on your college. It said 'The Radcliffe Infirmary.' "

The Radcliffe Infirmary is Oxford's largest hospital, and it is next door to Somerville College. Memory is fallible.

"Worlds Apart" is a powerful title to present to anyone involved in the writing of fantasy. It has a ring of The Other World, of echoes and shadows and things not quite within reach—and with those, for my metaphor-ridden mind, an implication of things unattainable or lost. One of the very first cuttings in the scrapbook I kept briefly when I was young is an article called "The Lost World," written for the Oxford university newspaper, Cherwell. Even at the age of nineteen I was already mourning something that was past. This article was a lament over the vanishing of magic and fairy tale. I could see my childhood vanishing into the distance and feel adulthood gobbling me up, and I wrote sorrowfully that the solitary bright spot in a dead world was Professor Tolkien's new epic, The Lord of the Rings. (It was a new epic in 1954; we were waiting for the last volume to come out.)

Well. The Lost World was so far from being lost that I was to spend the larger part of my life writing books about it, and Professor Tolkien's lonely bright spot became, of course, not only a best-seller but a kind of international cult. So much for the prescience of a nineteen-year-old. But that was in another country, and although the wench is not yet dead, she is altered. It's hard to be objective about Worlds Apart when I find myself back in Oxford, actually living here again for a few days. I came up to this university thirty-eight years ago, and it changed my life utterly. I was a naive, shy, practically mute eighteen-year-old, talented I suppose, but shackled by all the rigid insecurities of the English lower middle class. And here I was, plunged for three years into a privileged, challenging, protected hothouse of a world, and I emerged as a (relatively) confident, (relatively) grown-up writer. Oxford taught me how to write—not by giving me courses in "creative writing," perish the thought, but by teaching me how to read. Among other things.

I discovered libraries, real libraries—Bodley, the ultimate library. I discovered jazz, and sailing, and I watched Roger Bannister run the world's first four-minute mile, out at the Iffley

102

Road track. I discovered sex, of course; I wrote a mini-thesis about Shakespeare's Treatment of Time, and I managed to become the first woman to edit the university newspaper, *Cherwell*. The last of these accomplishments was technically against the rules. If you were an Oxford undergraduate in those days—perhaps still—you had a mentor, a nanny, called your moral tutor. He or she was supposed to guide your major decisions about life, and to keep you from major error. My moral tutor was a brilliant but remote scholar, and I had heard her fulminate about a former student who had taken to publishing newspaper articles. "Marghanita is prostituting her talent!" she'd cried. And here was I wanting not only to edit the newspaper but to do it in the term before Schools, Oxford's name for final examinations. I knew that if I asked my moral tutor's permission, she would say no—so I didn't ask. I just did it. And luckily she never read the newspaper, so she never knew.

I then went off to become a journalist for seven years, and I'm not sure she ever knew that either. But eventually when I was thirty-two I sent her a copy of *The Dark Is Rising*, and she wrote a nice letter back saying she'd always thought I had promise. Perhaps she liked the fact that I had tucked inside the story a quotation from the line written in Anglo-Saxon around King Alfred's Jewel, the greatest treasure of Oxford's Ashmolean Museum.

I dare say everyone looks back at some period in life as a golden time. Oxford was mine. And *I knew it*, at the time, which was an uncommon extra blessing. I would find myself waking up in the morning, or pulling on my gown, or walking down that amazing curve of the High Street, and hearing a small amazed voice in my head saying, *"I'm at Oxford."* Whatever might go wrong, however agonizing the love affair, however unnerving the examination, *I was at Oxford*. I've never felt so lucky, worked so hard and had so much fun, all at once.

And the golden world still hangs there in memory, shining, because it never had to acquire any dents or tarnish. Seven years after I came down from Oxford I married an American and moved to the U.S.A., and I've never spent a night in this university or city since—until last night. For my contemporaries who stayed in Britain, there was familiar old Oxford, still chugging away, eighty miles from London, changing yet remaining the same. It was connected at least tenuously to the fabric of their everyday lives, and if they didn't become dons themselves they knew people who did, or—in due course—they acquired children who started going up to do their own degrees. But for me Oxford was, is, in a time warp: it remains the magical world I entered just after my eighteenth birthday, and left just after my twenty-first. I can never go back to that world, even though here I am in Oxford now. Yet it isn't lost. It changed me, and so it is *in here* rather than *out there*. It's just—set apart.

For that is the powerful word, in our title. Apart. The Other World that's of value, in children's literature—or any other kind of literature, for that matter—doesn't have to be a shadowy fairyland, or a distant childhood. It is simply a world set apart. Separated, by geography or imagination. When we go into it, in the beginning, we have no idea of what we're doing. A reading child goes into a favorite story, which is read over and over again, as if he kept returning to a favorite place. He may indeed have a physical place as well: a corner of a room behind a curtain or a chair, or whatever. Some safe child-sized space, which may be of vast importance to him when he's four, even though he may not remember a thing about it when he's fourteen. It can be anywhere. For the English author Alan Garner this separate space was, of all things, a ceiling. He had three long serious illnesses when he was a child, diphtheria, meningitis and pneumonia, and so he spent months and years on his back in bed. Being both imaginative and ill, for much of the time he lived in the imaginary landscape he saw in the plaster above him; in its forests and hills, its cloudy sky, the road leading to its horizon. That was his world, and it molded his future. It's important to remember, as Garner says, that as children we accept our own circumstances as normality, having no concept of "things being other than they are found to be."

When I was about six years old, in wartime England, my brother and I were given a collection of cigarette cards, which had been put together by a friend of our parents in that mysterious world known as Before the War. (We were always hearing about Before the War: it was a vanished wonderland of freedom and plenty, filled with things we had never seen, like fountains and bananas.) A cigarette card was a picture, the size of a visiting card: a promotional gimmick which came in a packet of cigarettes. There were *sets* of them, so that people had to smoke themselves to death in order to acquire the cards to complete a set. Our favorite set showed an assortment of fantasy means of transport—and there was one card in particular which I came back to again and again.

The picture on this card showed a one-person vehicle, a huge glass sphere. I suppose it was a sphere within a sphere, because it rolled itself along and yet remained upright: the picture showed it bowling merrily through a field, with its lucky owner sitting inside, in the driver's seat. And as well as a seat, I always felt, he had in there a bed, a table, a stove, presumably even a mini-bathroom. All mod con. The sphere was a mobile home, a little round house. A little world.

I had dreams about that great glass ball. I would roll through life in it, in my dreams, self-contained, protected, safe. I was a very fearful child, as I remember, and the glass sphere—being, presumably, unbreakable—seemed to me to offer the perfect combination of independence, adventurousness and invulnerability. I knew it didn't exist, but I longed for it, fervently. Perhaps it would be invented by the time I grew up; perhaps I should find it waiting for me, in the future. I was too young to analyze my passion for this object, of course, which was just as well. You could hardly find a more striking example of the desire to return to the womb. And yet, perhaps there was more to it than that. . . .

A great many children find an equivalent of my rolling glass sphere, I think. Without knowing quite what they're doing, they put themselves inside a protective vehicle which will help them get through life without being damaged. It isn't round, however, it's generally rectangular; made not of glass but of paper. Many printed pages, between two hard covers. Or these days, more likely soft covers. This is likely to be the central image of this week of words: the image of the book, the story, as a small other world into which children—and adults too—can retreat, as a refuge from the cares and traumas of their lives. While they are inside it, reading, they have left the real world and are living in another. They have escaped. But if they are lucky, there's something else happening as well. They may be changed, just a little, by living in this world apart. They may take back a talisman from it, some small buried insight or idea that will stay with them forever, and help them in the hard matter of understanding and surviving their own world. It makes me think of that wonderful old comprehensive Everyman's Library published in the early years of this century by Dent and Dutton. The series encompassed all the best books in every field—or what Dent's editor Ernest Rhys thought were the best—and on the endpapers of each book was a quotation that could have been the book talking to its reader.

> Everyman, I will go with thee
> To be thy guide;
> In thy most need
> To be at thy side.

In the old morality play of *Everyman* those words are given to the character named Knowledge. We all need *him,* Lord knows.

One of the best things about the old Everyman books must have been their friendly size, which made them almost as portable as the modern paperback. My grandfather used to keep one in his pocket, so that he could dive inside it whenever he had a spare moment. This was good for his head, though it didn't do great things for his jackets. And now that we do have paperbacks, you can see Grandad's modern counterparts in buses and underground trains today, to some extent in the United States but more often in Britain, and above all in Japan: rows of travelers, sitting or standing, each reading a book, each inside his or her own little bubble of story.

When my children were young I particularly liked watching them reading in airplanes, on long transatlantic flights: there they sat, doubly encapsulated, held inside this cocoon of pressurized air zipping across the heavens at 350 miles an hour, but within *that* held too in another cocoon, woven by a writer's imagination.

On the whole, our motives for reading are probably more admirable when we're children than after we've grown up. Yes, the child is often retreating into a cocoon—but more often than not he or she is on a voyage of discovery, seeking out new worlds. Not us: we tend to look for the familiar. We know what we like. In the universe of books there are numbers of solar systems out there and most people stay firmly within one of them; they stick with thrillers, for instance, or biographies, or big meaty novels, the five-hundred-pagers spanning several generations.

The worlds within this last category, the big realistic novels, are true microcosms: filled with recognizable people and situations which will draw the reader in, make him (or her) smile or shiver, laugh or cry just as the people and situations do—less often—in his own life. They are more colorful than his own life, and they have the great virtue of being unreal, so that he gets all this lovely vicarious experience without any headaches: pleasure without responsibility. He joins the book's family—just for a little while. It's not unlike the experience of becoming part of an instant, temporary family at a Children's Literature New England institute. The enclosed, focused world of a conference can gobble you up, producing a sort of miniature hothouse version of the stresses and affections and dilemmas of the larger everyday world. Like the totally engaging novel whose plot you will forget within a month, it doesn't last, but it has its own intense valuable vitality while it's happening.

This phenomenon reaches its most extreme form in the

performing arts, as anyone knows who has lived through the full production process of a play, opera or ballet, or the shooting of a film. I've seldom been on a film set for more than a few days at a time, but once I was on location for the whole six-week shoot of a television film I'd written: part of the instant family, living through a ferocious range of human emotion from fury to love and back again. I have on my wall a souvenir of that time, a poster signed by all the members of the crew, with the most fulsome, fervent messages. "I shall never forget working with you . . ." they say. "Thank you for the most wonderful experience of my life . . . To my buddy, with great love and respect . . ." And I look at all the names of these people to whom I was so devoted, in our tight enclosed six-week world years ago, and I can hardly remember a thing about any one of them. Just as they probably remember nothing about me. If I had met them inside the world of a novel, at least I could reread the book.

But the slice-of-life novel is really not so much a world apart as an interlude—like the conference or the film set, the holiday hotel or the voyage by sea or air. You enter it, you live there for a while, you leave again. Perhaps it will alter you; usually it will not. I suspect that the book which takes you into a world apart must also *trouble* you, at least a little. And the troubling stays with you, like the grit in the oyster, and afterwards you are changed.

Consider, for instance, Ursula Le Guin's novel *Very Far Away from Anywhere Else,* a lovely book, though not perhaps the one that first springs to people's minds when they hear Mrs. Le Guin's name. This is a book about apartness. About Owen who is seventeen and amazingly good at math and science, and Natalie who is an eighteen-year-old musician and composer. They each have something that makes them different from everyone around them. Adolescence, as Owen says in the book, is the age "when kids begin to turn into people, and find out that they are alone"—and react in a way that's not friendly to individualists.

"I think what you mostly do when you find you really are alone is to panic," Owen says.

You rush to the opposite extreme and pack yourself into groups—clubs, teams, societies, types. You suddenly start dressing exactly like the others. It's a way of being invisible. The way you sew the patches on the holes in your blue jeans becomes incredibly important. If you do it wrong you're not with it. That's a peculiar phrase, you know? With it. With what? With them. With the others. All together. Safety in numbers. I'm not me. I'm a basketball letter. I'm a popular kid. I'm my friends' friend. I'm a black leather growth on a Honda. I'm a member. I'm a teenager. You can't see me, all you can see is us. We're safe.

And if We see You standing alone by yourself, if you're lucky we'll ignore you. If you're not lucky, we might throw rocks. Because we don't like people standing there with the wrong kind of patches on their jeans reminding us that we're each alone and none of us is safe.

You stand there with any kind of patches on your jeans today and they may throw rocks, because this book was published in 1976 and today—in my part of America, at any rate—patches aren't with it, unpatched holes are with it. Which just goes to prove what Mrs. Le Guin's Owen was saying.

Very Far Away from Anywhere Else is a kind of poem: a beautiful eighty-nine–page story about the way two people learn to cope with the fact that they must each live in a world apart from everyone else, if they are to fulfill the promise that is in them. I suppose it appeals to everyone who has ever had to survive a sensation of being different. (There was more than one reason why I wanted, when young, to roll through life inside that protective glass ball.) It is full of images that might well echo through this institute.

Haworth Parsonage, for instance.

Wuthering Heights was Natalie's favourite book, [says Owen,] and she knew a lot about the Brontë family, these four genius children living in a vicarage in a village on a moor in the middle of Nowhere,

England, a hundred and fifty years ago. Talk about being isolated! I read a biography of them she gave me; and I realized that maybe I thought I had been lonely, but my life had been an orgy of sociability, compared to those four.

The Brontë family as a world apart: Ursula Le Guin presents it to us on a plate, and we should keep it on our table this week. Then she moves on. On to Thorn, an invented country which Owen lives in as the Brontë children lived in theirs—in his imagination—during the years when he is changing from a child to a young adult. He says, of Thorn,

> It started out as a kingdom when I was twelve, but by the time I was fifteen or sixteen it had become a kind of free socialistic set-up, and so I had to work out all the history of how they got from autocracy to socialism, and also their relationships to other countries. They weren't at all friendly with Russia, China or the United States. In fact they traded only with Switzerland, Sweden and the Republic of San Marino. . . . Thorn was a very small country, on an island in the South Atlantic, only about sixty miles across, and a very long way away from anywhere else. . . .

Natalie is writing a wind quintet for Thorn, by the end of the book. She helps Owen come to terms with his necessary apartness, not least through sharing her awareness of her own. Perhaps this is really a book about talent and the acceptance of it, and the fact that learning how to work is one of the best ways of learning how to live. Natalie knows, and Owen recognizes, that she is set apart by her music. He says, of some songs she has written, "That's the way you really talk."

"Owen, you are the neatest person I ever knew," she says. "Nobody else understands that. I don't even know any other musicians who understand that. I can't really say anything. I can't even really be anything. Except in music. Maybe later. Maybe when I get good at music, maybe when I learn how to do that, then I'll be able to do some of the rest, too. Maybe I'll even become a human being."

And the two of them launch into adult life, and into the paradox that it's easier to survive apartness if you are connected to someone else. That even if the other person isn't actually around all the time, loving can carry you through the empty separate air, like the air pressure which keeps a fifty-ton airplane flying like a bird.

This is an achingly real book, but not an interlude. I wonder sometimes about the reactions of the children who read it. For any who feel even remotely akin to Owen and Natalie, it must be a glowing discovery. For the rest, who care more about having their jeans look the same as everyone else's jeans, I hope it's at least a little troubling, I hope it stays with them. Like the grit in the oyster, which is the necessary ingredient for—I quote from the motto of this institute—"comprehension of the self by the detour of the comprehension of the other."

On the face of it, the clearest example of a world apart is a book of fantasy. It separates the reader from reality, and takes him or her way apart, into magic. In the kind of fantasy which begins in an apparently normal world, there is a distinct moment when this shift takes place, like a signpost saying This Way Out. It's the moment when E. Nesbit's children find the Psammead, in *Five Children and It,* or when the Phoenix hatches from its egg in *The Phoenix and the Carpet;* when Alice goes through the looking-glass, when Lewis's children go through the wardrobe, or when Alan Garner's Roland walks through a door in a ruined Manchester church and is suddenly standing among boulders at the foot of a cliff in the land of Elidor.

Or my favorite paragraph in *The Children of Green Knowe,* when Mrs. Oldknow tells small Tolly that the three children whose portraits are on the walls, with whose lives he is so fascinated, all died with their mother three hundred years ago in the Great Plague, leaving their old grandmother bereft.

111

Mrs. Oldknow said, "It sounds very sad to say they all died, but it didn't really make so much difference. I expect the old grandmother soon found out they were still here."

Tolly was watching something travelling across the floor towards him. It was a marble, a glass one with coloured spirals in the middle. It stopped by his listless fingers. He picked it up. It was warm.

There's a moment that crosses this same kind of boundary in my own book *The Dark Is Rising*, when the boy Will is carried away by a white horse from a danger not yet named, and the horse, galloping through the countryside, takes off and rides up into the sky. Into fantasy. I love those moments when we are transported into another world—which is no doubt why I write the kind of fantasy which contains them. It's probably related to another obsession of mine that I'm forever using as an analogy: that breathtaking moment in the theater when the house lights have gone down, the voices have hushed, and the curtain begins to go up. Into fantasy.

(I have to add that I was almost cured of this obsession once when I was standing at the back of the stalls for a performance of a play I'd written, and as the house lights began to dim, my companion said in my ear, "Just think—it's like eight hundred people opening a book of yours, all at once." And I found this image so terrifying that I had to leave, instantly. Eight hundred books are much more frightening than one stage. At least in the theater you have the chance of blaming the actors, if people don't like the play.)

Fantasy writers born in America tend, for whatever reason, to be more direct than those born in Britain. They take you straight to their world apart: from the first page, you are not in our own world but in Ursula Le Guin's Earthsea, Anne McCaffrey's Pern, Lloyd Alexander's Prydain. Or for that matter, just to disprove my own generalization about nationality, Professor Tolkien's Middle-earth. This brand of fantasy could be said to be the ultimate in separation: how much further from reality can you get than to be

112

in a different universe, a different time, belonging to a different species?

But it's an illusion. Fantasy, of whatever kind, may seem to be picking you up and carrying you away but in fact it's taking you right back home. All fantasy involves metaphor. I once called a piece I'd written about it "Escaping into Ourselves"—and that's precisely what we're doing in this kind of fiction, both of us, writer and reader. The writer takes the images, themes, characters which come bubbling up from his—or her—unconscious mind (the ultimate world apart), and puts them into his story. There they stay, part of the fabric, and like radioactive elements they give off signals about the meaning of the story, the nature of its metaphor. But because they come from the unconscious, the writer himself generally doesn't know what these signals are. He may not even know they are there.

Quite often the reader doesn't either. But his—or her—own unconscious mind has its own little Geiger counter. Ticking away as he reads, it picks up these signals from the story and takes them in, without the reader having consciously recognized them at all. This is a totally nonrational process. It has nothing to do with critical judgments; it's as instinctive and uncontrollable as being in love. The rational mind, probably adult, may read Mary Norton's books about those very small creatures the Borrowers in a thoroughly objective manner. It will admire the ingenuity which turns a nutshell into a cup, a soapdish into a dinghy, a knitting-needle into a punt-pole. It will be entertained by the story, and draw parallels with Gulliver and the Lilliputians. But it won't necessarily make the instinctive unconscious connection through which the child reader, being small, understands that these are books about the tensions and delights of living as a small person in a large world. The analytical mind makes more noise than the imagination. It drowns out those signals from the unconscious. Children, today, make the best readers of fantasy, because children, as C. S. Lewis observed a long time ago, read only to enjoy.

I am a jack-of-all-trades, as an author; I've spent thirty years responding, probably unwisely, to the challenges of different forms. But fantasy is my natural habitat. It's the kind of writing I am best at, I think. I've seldom deliberately chosen it; it simply tends to take over. The first book I wrote that was published for children didn't set out to be a fantasy at all; it was supposed to be an adventure story, but magic began glimmering through it before I had reached the end of Chapter Two. This has been happening at intervals ever since, as if my imagination were refusing ever to rely on straightforward reality. Often, when I begin to think about an idea for a book, it's as though I were sitting at a concert, hearing a new orchestral piece of music; I relax into the sweep of strings and woodwind, percussion and brass, convinced that I am listening to the first theme of the first movement of a symphony. But sooner or later, soft as faraway bells, the notes of the piano come creeping in. There's the same theme, simple, crystalline, then growing, growing until great chords are crashing away and intertwining with the orchestra—and lo, after all it's not a symphony, yet again it's a concerto. With fantasy as the solo instrument, taking over the piece of music, making its very specific magic. Showing off, you might say.

Why? Why is it that my imagination, my world apart, chooses to express itself fully only in fantasy? Penelope Farmer grappled with the question in a talk about form, seventeen years ago; she said, "I am asked why, as a writer for children, I do not produce nice, solid, useful novels on the problem of the adopted child, or aimed at the reluctant reader, and so forth, instead of highly symbolic (according to some reviewers) obscure (according to others)—anyway, *difficult* fantasies. Very simply, because I cannot. It is the same for everyone—no one can express himself effectively except in ways and forms suited to him. . . ." When she tried to write in other, more realistic forms, she said,

> I lose the simplest verbal competence. . . . Whereas writing within my usual form, fantasy, given time and given a good idea, I feel sometimes

114

a kind of fluency and ease. And as for form, I scarcely have to look for it. . . . It pushes up from some unknown part of my mind, I can feel it happening, watch it slowly, gradually, fall neatly into place.

. . . It seems that I need symbols and images. . . . Without those images, I cannot frame my idea and expand it into narrative. . . . For me the extraordinary is a means of looking at people sideways and finding out more about them—and me.

Which is another way of saying that she, and I, are escaping into ourselves. Writing is one of the loneliest professions in the world because it has to be practiced in this very separate private world, in *here*. Not in the mind; in the imagination. And I think it is possible that the writing of fantasy is the loneliest job of the lot, since you have to go further inside. You have to make so close a connection with the unconscious that the unbiddable door will open and the images fly out, like birds. It's not unlike writing poetry.

It makes you superstitious. Most writers indulge in small private rituals to start themselves writing each day, and I find that when I'm working on a fantasy I'm even more ludicrously twitchy than usual. The very first half hour at the desk has nothing much to do with fantasy or even ritual: it's what J. B. Priestley used to call "sharpening pencils"—the business of doing absolutely everything you can think of to put off the moment of starting work. You make another cup of coffee. You find a telephone call that must be made, a letter that must be answered. You *do* sharpen pencils. You look at the plant on the windowsill and decide this is just the time to water it, or fertilize it, or prune it. Maybe it's even time to repot it. You hunt for the houseplant book, and look this up, and it says severely that this kind of plant enjoys being pot-bound and should never be repotted. So you turn to the bowl of paper clips on the desk, and find that safety pins and pennies and buttons have found their way in, so of course you really ought to sort out the paper clips. . . .

Finally guilt drives you to the manuscript—and that's when the

115

real ritual begins. (I should go back to the first person, because in this respect everyone's different.) I have to start by reading. I read a lot of what I've already written, probably two or three chapters, even though I already know it all by heart. I read the notes I made to myself the day before when I stopped writing— those were the end-of-the-day ritual, to help with the starting of the next. During this process I've picked up one of the toys scattered around my study, and my fingers are half-consciously playing with it: a shell, a smooth sea-washed pebble from an island beach, a chunky ceramic owl from Sweden, a little stone wombat from Australia. I read the last chapter again. I wander to a bookshelf and read a page of something vaguely related to my fantasy: Eliot's *Quartets*, maybe, or de la Mare's notes to *Come Hither*. I have even been known to blow bubbles, from a little tube that sits on my desk, and to sit staring at the colors that swirl over their brief surfaces. This is the moment someone else usually chooses to come into the room, and I can become very irritable if they don't appreciate that they are observing a writer seriously at work.

What I'm doing, of course, is taking myself out of the world I'm in, and trying to find my way back into the world apart. Once I've managed that, I am inside the book that I'm writing, and am *seeing* it, so vividly that I do not see what I'm actually staring at: the wall, or the typewriter, or the tree outside the window. I suppose it is a variety of trance state, though that's a perilous word. It makes one think of poor Coleridge, waking from an opium-induced sleep with two hundred glowing lines of *Kubla Khan* in his head, being interrupted by a person from Porlock when he'd written down only about ten of them, and finding, when the person had gone, that he'd forgotten all the rest. Trance is fragile.

The world of the imagination is not fragile, not once you've reached it, but because it is set apart you can never be *sure* of reaching it. It seems very curious to be standing here in the university which tried to teach me reason, and confessing to

116

uncertainty and superstition of a kind which would have appalled my tutor. Reason, however, is singularly unhelpful to a novelist except in a few specialized situations, like the matter of choosing a publisher, or arguing points of English grammar with a copy editor. The imagination is not reasonable—or tangible, or visible, or obedient. It's an island out in the ocean, which often seems to retreat as you sail toward it. Sometimes it vanishes altogether, mirage-like, and nothing can be done to bring it back within reach. This produces a bad day during which you write nothing of value and have to wait till tomorrow and start again.

We cast spells to find our way into the unconscious mind, and the imagination that lives there, because we know that's the only way to get into a place where magic is made. "Open sesame!" I am shouting, silently, desperately to the door of my imagination, as I play with the pebble I found on a distant island beach, as I stare at the wall.

Our readers believe that the process is magical too. That's why they say to us in that bemused, incredulous, faintly envious way, "Where do you get your ideas?" It always sounds like a dinner guest contemplating the salad, asking a hostess to reveal the name of some special shop. "Where do you get your tomatoes?"

The answer might well be the same whether it's tomatoes or ideas. "I grow them. In my garden." If the subject is ideas, they know that it's a magic garden. They've been there, transported to it while they read the book. Though they didn't have to go through all the same palaver to get there that we did; all they had to do was to open the cover. They come into this place by reading words on paper, nothing more. They've been transported to separate worlds before in the theater, or the cinema, sometimes even in front of the television set, but there they were witnessing reproductions of things happening, watching actors, through the fourth wall. In the book, the magic is all in the words on paper, taking them into the writer's imagination. Words on paper. Isn't that extraordinary? The Russian director Aleksandr Sokurov just made a new film of *Madame Bovary,* and spoke of it with proper but uncommon humility. "The film is the child of literature, and not the father," he said, in an interview. "It will never be able to replace the silent and private dialogue between reader and book."

Six weeks ago I was speaking at another children's book conference, a long way away, called "Literature and Hawaii's Children." It took place on the island of Oahu and then, a smaller repeat performance, on Hawaii, also known as The Big Island. This is the home of Pele, goddess of fire, and of two of the world's most active volcanoes: Mauna Loa, which had a spectacular eruption in 1984, and Kilauea, which has been erupting continuously since 1983. My editor, Margaret McElderry, was with me, and on our one day off she came to me, bright-eyed, waving a leaflet that advertised helicopter flights over the volcano Kilauea.

I looked at the leaflet, and I thought very superstitious thoughts about the goddess Pele. "I can't afford it," I said.

Margaret McElderry is a strong-minded lady. She said, "We're going. I didn't give you a birthday present this year. This is it."

So up we went in a helicopter, over the dead black lava fields stretching to the sea, over steaming cracks and vents, over huge creeping fingers of new hot lava—suitably called in Hawaiian, which is a language full of hesitations, *'a'a*. To the crater, around which—and into which—we swooped like a small rash bird.

The helicopter felt like a sturdy little refuge, but it grew warm. I was so busy taking photographs, and peering through the smoke and fumes at the glowing red heart of the volcano, that I didn't hear the echoes that were beginning to murmur out of my unconscious mind.

Then we banked away from the crater, and up through ragged white cliffs and valleys of cloud. Away from the urgency of the volcano, through this tranquil, mounded sky, with glimpses of black and eventually green fields beneath our feet. They were *literally* beneath our feet; I looked down past my shoes to see them. It was a very small helicopter, and we were sitting surrounded by glass in its nose, next to the pilot. There was glass on either side of us and in front of us, glass above us and glass below us.

I had seen this before, somewhere, a long time ago.

It was as if we were sitting inside a glass ball.

If you have the cast of mind of a fantasy writer, and if you pay attention to the life you are living, once in a while you will find yourself bang in the middle of a metaphor. Here I was, suddenly, inside the huge glass sphere that had haunted me when I was young. Inside the picture from the cigarette card.

I was in my world apart: the writer's imagination, the child's book. But I knew more about its value now than I had before. It wasn't an escape really, nor a refuge. It stood for freedom, and discovery, and wonder. The best thing about it wasn't that it was safe, but that it was *flying*.

WHO ARE THE CHILDREN?
The Zena Sutherland Lecture for 1995,
given at the Chicago Public Library

One of the more irritating things about authors published for children is their habit of claiming that they don't write for children. We all say it, probably too often. I once gave a talk in which I said it eleven times, ten of them quotations from other authors. The disclaimer seems particularly disingenuous and infuriating to our publishers, whose lives are devoted to getting these books-not-written-for-children to their proper readers—who *are* children.

But it's true nonetheless. If you write self-consciously *for* children, there's a terrible danger that you will end up writing down to them. The worst children's books do just that. Early Victorian children's books did it all the time. Consider for instance a book published in London in 1828: *The Child's Instructor,* "intended as a first book, for children, with superior engravings," written by "a fellow of the Royal Society" who clearly wanted to be anonymous.

One of the superior engravings shows two little boys beside a pond, each holding a model boat, and the text underneath reads,

> Take care little George and do not fall into the water. He appears very much pleased with his boat, and well he may be, as it was given him for being a good boy and learning his lesson.

His brother who had a present from his uncle, wishes to launch his vessel also, but he is very patient, waiting till his brother shall get out of the way.

How pleasant it is to see brothers and sisters agree and love one another, and always give way to each other rather than contend and be fretful!

Well, yes, it may be pleasant, but that's no way to write for children. It was much later in the nineteenth century—about seventy years later—before children began to hear from authors like E. Nesbit, who for all her racism and snobbery did at least manage to talk to them as if they were people. Here she is at the beginning of *The Phoenix and the Carpet,* just after the Bastable children, Anthea, Cyril, Robert and Jane, have found a peculiar egg-shaped stone rolled up in the second-hand carpet bought for their nursery. These are not virtuous and patient children—they wrecked the first carpet by lighting fireworks on it. This time, they manage to knock the strange stone egg into the fire. Robert reaches for the poker, but Anthea stops him. "Look at it!" she says. "Look! Look!"

And now I'm quoting:

For the egg was now red hot, and inside it something was moving. Next moment there was a soft cracking sound; the egg burst in two and out of it came a flame-coloured bird. It rested a moment among the flames, and as it rested there the four children could see it growing bigger and bigger under their eyes.

The bird rose in its nest of fire, stretched its wings, and flew out into the room. It flew round and round, and round again, and where it passed the air was warm. Then it perched on the fender. The children looked at each other. Then Cyril put out a hand to the bird. It put its head on one side and looked up at him, as you may have seen a parrot do when it is just going to speak, so that the children were hardly astonished at all when it said, "Be careful, I am not nearly cool yet."

They were not astonished, but they were very, very much interested.

121

Now that's writing. It's not quite the way most of us write today, but it tells its story, vividly, conversationally, without condescension. "And where it passed, the air was warm. . . ."—when she wrote that line, I guarantee you she wasn't thinking about who would read it, she was just *there*. And as a result the audience is caught up in experiencing the Phoenix, just as she was. If instead you write coolly and carefully for children as if they were an inferior race of limited intelligence, they will not only resent you, they won't read you. I often wonder whether a single early Victorian child ever read one of those pre-Nesbit Improving Texts, unless compelled to by a parent or a nanny.

The successors to E. Nesbit are those of us on the modern children's book lists, and we are able to write without paying any attention to the age of our audience. And by the same token they don't feel separated from us by age. I suppose they take it for granted that we're adults, but we're simply the storytellers, and they the audience. We communicate.

I sometimes feel it necessary to remind people, vigorously, that children do not belong to a separate race; they are *us*, not yet wearing our heavy jacket of Time. Book marketing people use that enigmatic term Young Adult for a particular age-group, from twelve on up—but all children are young adults, just as all puppies are young dogs. Many things change as we grow up, some for the better and some for the worse, but a few do not, and one of them is the imagination. In that respect, this senior author standing before you is still the eight-year-old who in the 1940s was reading Eleanor Farjeon, Arthur Ransome, Malcolm Saville, and skipping through Charles Dickens; I still have the same automatic response to fairy tale, folktale, myth, to verse, music and theater. The imagination is still the same.

I don't know whether anyone has ever tried to chart the chronological development of the imagination, but I would guess that it's fully grown by about the age of six. Or at the very latest, eight. It's formed by then, it will not get larger, or more lively, or more responsive. Age and education and experience can direct it and feed it, but they won't alter its quality. They can however starve the imagination; they can even kill it. That's why such a huge responsibility rests on the shoulders of parents, teachers and children's librarians, the keepers of the imaginative flame in an increasingly drafty world. If—with their help—the imagination does remain intact, it survives in the adult just as it was in the child: a little stiffer and less fertile perhaps, like the body, but essentially the same. And *that* is the fundamental link between the child and the so-called children's author. One full-grown imagination is speaking to another.

People are formed by more things than their imaginative capacity, of course. They belong to their own time. My imagination may be much the same as it was when I was eight, but the world isn't. The zeitgeist, the spirit of the age, has changed. The child out of whom I write lived in a world where a Nazi bomb could fall from the sky and obliterate you any day or night; where everything was in short supply except fear; where there was no television, and only the occasional movie. You read a lot, you did your sums by mental arithmetic, you wrote with a pencil or a fountain pen, and you filled up even the inside covers of your exercise book.

That's fifty years ago. Half a century. When I was that child, I couldn't imagine living so long.

Today, the child whom I hope to reach lives in a world which is still full of violence and fear, God knows, but in which there are far more *things:* more food, more toys, more "consumer goods." She/he lives in a materialistic society in which television advertising constantly fuels the materialism, and television itself fills her head with ephemeral images—the average child between two and eleven years old is said to watch four hours a day, a statistic which I hope is wrong, but probably isn't. Our child today is told stories more often through movies and videos than through books; the pictures in her mind are frequently those she sees on a screen, rather than the pictures her imagination makes from words she has read or heard. She/he has a calculator to help with math, and is taught in school how to use a computer. (Between this child and the child I was, typewriters have come and gone.) Screens increasingly play a larger part in her leisure and learning than the printed page does; the picture book now has a serious rival in the interactive CD-ROM.

I live in this world too, of course. I too am beset with screens. In my last book, *The Boggart*, computer screens played a major part in the plot. I should like to claim that this was the result of a shrewd and deliberate choice; the act of an aging author plugging into the zeitgeist in order to connect with the concerns of the modern child. But it wasn't. It was an accident. All I knew was that I wanted to write a book about an ancient creature, the trick-playing, shape-shifting boggart who is one of the minor Old Things of Britain; I wanted to tell the story of what might happen if a boggart were brought by chance across the Atlantic to the New World, to play his tricks there. So I started writing (in longhand, as I still do at first) and it just so chanced that I was at the time having a love affair with my third computer, a lovely Macintosh racehorse which deserves a better jockey than me. Before I quite knew what was happening, the computer had insinuated itself into my story—not through a conscious choice, but because, like everything else that feeds an author's ideas, its image had snuggled down to lie in wait in my unconscious mind.

My publishers are very consciously aware of the world of the modern child. They have to be: they're trying to sell him/her books—that is, to the extent that children's books are actually bought by children, rather than parents and aunts and uncles, librarians and teachers. In Britain, both paperback and hardback publishers of the five-book *Dark Is Rising* sequence, Penguin/Puffin and The Bodley Head, brought out new editions last year, commissioning ten new jackets in the process. Twelve jackets, actually, because each publisher also happens to be doing a sort of Junior Classics list, and the single book called *The Dark Is Rising* is on each of these.

So one by one these twelve new jackets arrived on my desk, and they were startling, to say the least. They all looked like something from a horror science-fiction list. The first one was so lurid that when a British children's book magazine published the artwork on its cover, several adult readers attacked the editor for sensationalism.

I said to the paperback art editor, "Why the horrific jackets?"

"Horror is very big at the moment," she said. "That's what they're all buying."

I said, "But what happens when they start reading the book they've bought, and find out that it's fantasy, not horror?"

She smiled a charming smile, and she said, "Well, after the first page or two we hope you'll have grabbed them."

This was an excellent way of disarming an author, but not illuminating as a comment on today's child. The new jackets are a time-honored marketing ploy: you put the breakfast cereal in a bright new box, and you hope children will happily eat it even after they find it's still cornflakes. But who are those children? Are they us? Are we them? Or are they different, as a nymph is different from a dragonfly?

Many years ago I took part in a conference called "Innocence and Experience" which did try to address this question. Nina Bawden quoted one of the characters in her book *Carrie's War*, a boy called Albert. "It's a fearful handicap being a child," said Albert. "You can never make anything happen." And youth does imply a low place on the ladder of life, before the acquisition of power. It's another version of that famous *bon mot* that says: yes, the rich are different from us, they have more money. Yes, the old are different from the young; they've lived longer.

"Children are not less intelligent than we are," said Nina Bawden, "but they lack experience."

"Children explore," said Joan Aiken. "Because they instinctively know they don't yet have a fund of experience to draw on."

And Paula Fox said, "Children have not been in the world as long as adults. They may have every kind of virtue, great wit, and imagination, but they don't have judgment. In fact, it takes a long time for any of us to have a little judgment."

Oh yes. A long time—far too long.

But some people feel that the acquisition of judgment and experience sets up a barrier between children and adults as powerful as the Berlin Wall. I've been haunted for years by something Penelope Lively said at that conference, probably because I admire her so enormously and was startled to find myself convinced that she was wrong. "Children live in another country," said Penelope,

> and although it is one we have all passed through, to pass beyond it is to have lost, irretrievably I believe, its language and its beliefs. We have lost the sense of a continuous present and have moved into an awareness of what has been and what is yet to be and of our own situation in relation to time—both personal time as the context of a life and collective time, history.

She went on:

> I do not believe it is possible for an adult to recover the vision of childhood. You write for children, as an adult, with the expanded understanding of experience, and there is no way in which this understanding can be shed.

I don't think that's true: not for writers. Maybe it's true for child psychologists: they have to *study* children, to analyze their behavior, a very distancing process. In *The Uses of Enchantment*, Bruno Bettelheim tells how a three-year-old girl once asked the legendary psychologist Jean Piaget a question about an elephant's wings.

Piaget shook his head. "Elephants don't fly," he said.

"Yes they do," said the little girl. "I've seen them."

To which Piaget replied, with remarkable Swiss stolidity, "You must be joking."

The trouble here, said Bettelheim, was that the little girl was instinctively using fantasy, probably as an unconscious expression of something that was bothering her. (Why were her elephants in such a hurry that they were flying? Were they trying to escape from something?) Whereas Piaget was being rational. (Real elephants don't fly.) "This is the tragedy of so much 'child psychology,'" said Bettelheim. "Its findings are correct and important, but do not benefit the child. Psychological discoveries aid the adult in comprehending the child from within an adult's frame of reference. But such adult understanding of a child's mind often increases the gap between them."

Here are two child psychologists disagreeing with each other, which is fun, but both doing it from the other side of that gap— firmly, irredeemably grown up. (Bettelheim, after all, is the man who described *Hansel and Gretel* as a story about oral fixation symbolically turned into cannibalism, and Little Red Riding Hood as a girl giving in to the temptations of her id.) These firmly grown-up people are fascinated by childhood, and children are the life's work on which they bring to bear all their adult experience and understanding. They have that much in common with the preschool teacher, who can communicate with small children not because she or he is childish, but because she has a gift for combining an unusual amount of patience and restraint with the sophisticated, trained judgments of an adult.

Not all adults have this patience; not even all artists. Some artists have none whatsoever, like the brilliant but monstrous English novelist Evelyn Waugh, who had six children and once wrote about them to a friend, "I abhor their company, because I can only regard children as defective adults, hate their physical ineptitude, find their jokes flat and monotonous." From his great self-imposed distance, I don't think Evelyn Waugh ever wrote a children's book.

To some degree, of course, no member of the human race ever completely grows up. Life is not an automatic moving staircase to maturity and wisdom; if it were, Freud would never have been published and the psychiatric profession would have nothing to do. Elements of the child-self remain in all adults, and take over at the most disconcerting moments. A friend of mine died some years ago in her eighties, and the reaction of her middle-aged children was extraordinary: out of their mourning they started producing detailed reminiscences of childhood neglect, reproachful, bitter, even angry. This was indistinct stuff cobwebbed by memory, long-buried in the past; why did it come flooding out now? Because somewhere inside, they were still children and their mother had left them. They were angry with her because they loved her, and she had died.

If I live long enough, I shall one day write a book about my own mother and father, whom I adored, but whom I have not been able to think about in detail, for any length of time, since the year when they died within six weeks of each other. That was *fifteen years ago* in 1980, but the child part of me is still paralyzed in mourning. I have all their letters from the day I first left home to go to college; decades of letters, but I haven't yet been able to reread a word of them—I who live by words. Even at my age, that part of me still hasn't coped with the hurt, and is still waiting to grow up.

This kind of residual childishness helps one to appreciate the ferocity of the basic emotions that we feel in childhood, starting presumably with that traumatic moment of birth. Loss, need, love, hunger, delight, grief, rage, laughter, pain—they're with us from the beginning to the end. But they don't make a bridge between the child and the adult understanding, over that abyss that Penelope Lively claimed was unbridgeable.

I have a confession to make, about a smaller kind of abyss: I really don't know how to behave with children. I had a wonderful time with my own two, from when they were babies and all through childhood, and indeed still, today. But that's parenthood, that's different (unless you're Evelyn Waugh). Put me with a group of unfamiliar children, and I don't know what to do. I didn't even when I was a young mother, and as a result I used to think up all kinds of elaborate birthday treats for my Jonathan and Kate to avoid having to cope with the social logistics of a birthday party. They were *deprived* of parties, except on rare and effortful occasions. When Jonathan later spent four rambunctious years in a fraternity house at Cornell, it occurred to me that he was probably trying to catch up.

I still have this same handicap. I talk on rare occasions to adult audiences, but hardly ever to children; I don't Do Schools, as we say in the trade. I pretend that this is because my five best-known books, *The Dark Is Rising* sequence, are published for readers too old to want classroom visits, but the truth is that I'm scared stiff of trying to communicate with those rows of challenging young faces. I am consumed with envy of the friends I've watched working magic on young audiences: John Langstaff making them sing, Ashley Bryan holding them openmouthed with performances of poems, Gerald McDermott drawing them instant pictures at a large easel with a flashing crayon.

I can't do any of those things; I can only talk to them, and I haven't the remotest idea what to say, or more important, how to say it. The most inexperienced grade-school teacher knows better than I do how to grab the attention of a class of children, and make them want to listen. For decades I used to brood over this shameful secret of mine. *They call you a children's author,* I used to think miserably. *They give you prizes for it. What would they say if they could see you turn into a mumbling jelly in front of a bunch of real kids?*

Then one day a few years ago, I had to give a lecture in Kentucky, and the morning before I was to speak, it was sprung upon me that I was also expected to talk to an audience of children at the local library. "It won't take more than an hour or so," said my keeper, merrily driving me off to the library. "And they're all looking forward to it so much—they've given up their Saturday morning specially!"

Now I'm not capable of saying anything to anybody in public

without writing it down first. It took ten days of solid work before I could deliver the speech written on these pages. And there I was in Kentucky with no time at all, gibbering with fright; suddenly finding myself sitting on a chair in a big room jammed with maybe a hundred and fifty children, aged from fifteen down to about three. There weren't many chairs, and most of the children were squirming on the floor. The librarian introduced me, and I stared at them in horror and started stumbling through a kind of potted autobiography. They listened politely enough, but you could see the fidgets, and hear the coughs. After a while I couldn't bear it any longer, and I took refuge in reading to them.

I had a galley proof of *The Boggart* with me, which I'd been correcting on the plane, and on the way into the library I'd stolen the librarian's copy of my latest picture book, *Matthew's Dragon*. So I started to read to them from *The Boggart* and suddenly the room took on that lovely prickling silence that tells you when an audience is really listening. And because I had no microphone and I haven't a loud voice, they sat very still, so that they could hear.

After that I read them *Matthew's Dragon*, displaying the pictures as I went, and a wonderful thing happened. I was Projecting a little better by now, and they were still listening, and from the front row of the children sitting on the floor, a little girl, about four years old I guess, began inching herself toward me. She had straggly blonde hair and a pale little face, and big eyes fixed on me, and as the story went on she just kept quietly shunting herself forward on her hands at intervals, listening. At first I thought she must be a shortsighted kid who wanted a better look at the pictures, but by coming close she couldn't see the pictures at all, because I was holding the book up high, over her head and mine, every time I turned a page. But she kept coming, until her head was resting against my knee.

I think the truth was that she wanted to get inside the story.

So I finished reading, with my hand on the small blonde head, and afterward we had a very lively question time and were all, indeed, communicating. But it was the story, and the small entranced girl, that had brought us together. The link between the imagination of the storyteller, and the imagination of the reader—in this case the listener. Maybe I can't chat away to small children in the flesh, but I can reach their imaginations. As Ellen Raskin once said, "I can write about images from my own childhood for children today. I wasn't sure I could do this, but there was no way out; I had to use the images from my own childhood, because the child I was is the only child I really know."

The child I was is the only child I really know. That's it. I can still feel what it was like to be that child of the 1940s from inside; I am still the same mixture of insecurity and determination, shyness and arrogance, curiosity and fear. I have the same talent she had; the same imagination. I write for her, for that child, and so it is true when I say I write for myself. And equally true when I say I don't write for children, not for those rows of alarming unpredictable faces. But behind the faces, there are the imaginations like mine.

Who are the children? That's who they are: the keepers of the imagination, of the one part of us which can survive unchanged all through life. As people, they will certainly change, as dramatically as the seedling which grows up to be a tree. The high voices will grow deep, the chubby cheeks become fine-boned; the skin will wrinkle and the hair drop off the head. Well, some of it. As for the personalities, you only have to think of any high school or college reunion you may have attended to remember how some of those will change. But the quality of the imagination, especially in any child who grows up to be an artist, will remain a kind of talisman that links him or her to every child who will come after.

The children *are* us. I don't have much faith in the value of hypnotic regression, that technique for sending people back to re-experience their childhoods; it seems to me to be often alarmingly overdone, dredging up so much buried child abuse that you'd think the whole country was founded on incest. But the principle remains valid: the child is father of the man, mother of the woman. I write out of the imagination I already had yesterday, and today's children read—and will go on reading, and maybe writing too—out of the imaginations they will carry into tomorrow.

And because they are today's children, living in the age of the screen, they need all the help we can give them. In the development of the imagination, there is no substitute for the freshness of the image that a child creates himself, as a response to words. Words stretch the muscles of the imagination. Continual placid acceptance of ready-made visual images turns the imagination into a couch potato. Perhaps you noticed the recent Department of Education report announcing that only one-third of all American high school seniors are proficient readers. *Two-thirds* of our high school graduates can't read well. Because, said the Secretary of Education, children are spending "too much time watching mind-numbing television."

Child or adult, our eyes see differently if they feed, and are fed by, an alert imagination. The painter-poet William Blake, when he was a child, saw on Peckham Rye a tree full not of birds but of angels. (*He* would have understood the little girl who saw elephants flying.) "I know," said Blake after he had grown up, "that this world is a world of imagination and vision. I see everything I paint in this world, but everybody does not see alike. . . . The tree which moves some to tears of joy is in the eyes of others only a green thing which stands in the way. . . . Some scarce see Nature at all. But to the eyes of the man of imagination, Nature is Imagination itself."

I should like you to listen to a small story from Walter de la Mare's anthology *Come Hither,* a wonderful book in which the notes suggested by poems are as magical as the poems themselves. I mean it to tug at your imagination. Like William Blake's angels, it's set on Peckham Rye—a rye is a common, and this one, in London, has been common land since time immemorial.

In the year 1872, an old lady might have been seen driving across the Rye in her silvery carriage; and she came to where, under a flowering tree, sat a small boy—the locks of hair upon his head like sheaves of cowslips, his eyes like speedwells, and he in very bright clothes. And he was a-laughing up into the tree.

She stopped her carriage and said to him almost as if she were more angry than happy, 'What are you laughing at, child?'

And he said, 'At the sparrows, ma'am.'

'Mere sparrows!' says she. 'But why?'

'Because they were saying,' says he, 'here comes across the Rye a blind old horse, a blind old coachman and a blind old woman.'

'But I am not blind,' says she.

'Nor are they not *mere* sparrows,' said the child.

And at that the old lady was looking out of her carriage at no child, but at a small bush, in bud, of golden gorse.

It's only people like that imperceptive old woman who think of children as a separate race, living in a lost country. Not only can she not enter the small boy's mind, share his delight, and see through his eyes; by the end, she can't see him at all. I think of that small boy, and of my small blonde girl in Kentucky, as the child I was and still am, keeper of the imagination out of which I write. He is you too. There are people who are blind to the imagination, but they are not the kind of people who come to listen to the Zena Sutherland lecture.

I am not one of those gloomy prophets who fear that the Electronic Revolution is going to be the death of the book. There are words on all those computer screens as well as images, and once they are fed through the printer they become our old familiar friend, the written word. Some electronic advances have caused unfortunate gaps; for anyone who used card catalogs as often as I did, the computer is a slow and clumsy substitute, and it's no consolation at all that it can plug me into the contents of other libraries all round my town or country. The card catalog has gone the way of the railroad track, and will one day be just as bitterly regretted. Books, however, can and will co-exist with screens—though not without care and protection from those of us who know their value. And that means, above all, encouraging children to read. Their imaginations must be fed and nurtured—and occasionally something more than their imaginations as well.

Once in a great while, if you write books for children, a very particular kind of letter turns up in the mail. Most of the letters come from kids who are Doing You in Class, or Need Information for a book report, or have been forced to Write to an Author—or who just felt like writing because they enjoyed a book and wanted to say so. But sometimes there's a serious, passionate one who says, quite literally, *your book changed my life.* They're generally older, in their twenties, and they're looking back and saying, hey, you did something for me, thank you. These letters are of course quite marvelous for an author to have—but beyond that, they are important for all of us to remember, as a shining beacon to the importance of books.

Graham Greene once wrote, in an essay called "The Lost Childhood,"

> Perhaps it is only in childhood that books have any deep influence on our lives. In later life we admire, we are entertained, we may modify some views we already hold, but we are more likely to find in books merely a confirmation of what is in our minds already; as in a love affair it is our own features that we see reflected flatteringly back.
>
> But in childhood all books are books of divination, telling us about the future, and like the fortune teller who sees a long journey in the cards or death by water they influence the future. I suppose that is why books excited us so much. What do we ever get nowadays from reading to equal the excitement and the revelation in those first fourteen years? . . . It is in those early years that I would look for the crisis, the moment when life took a new slant in its journey towards death.

• • •

The crisis for Graham Green was a matter of a particular book, *The Viper of Milan,* by Marjorie Bowen, which he read when he was about fourteen. Something about its style, its subject, its mood totally took hold of him. When he took that book from the shelf, he said, "the future for better or worse really struck. From that moment I began to write. All the other possible futures slid away: the potential civil servant, the don, the clerk had to look for other incarnations." And he went on writing.

"Crisis" is perhaps overdramatic, as a word to express the feeling "your book changed my life." But it will do. Of the young people who wrote me those particular letters, over the years, a few kept in touch. Three of them said they were led by *The Dark Is Rising* books to study Welsh, not just here but in Wales, and now they're back and one of them is a writer and two are university teachers. One boy said simply, "Your books helped me to find myself, as nothing else could," and he went off from Stanford to the Far East for two years, and then to the Kennedy School of Government at Harvard, and is now building public housing in San Francisco.

There's an English boy who's in sports medicine in Liverpool; don't ask me how *The Dark Is Rising* put him there but he says it did. There's a linguistics major from Berkeley who's training to be a children's librarian; there are two or three struggling screenwriters, and there's a musician who just sent me her first CD, with a letter that said, "*The Grey King* especially had a tremendous influence on my life. It inspired my interest in Celtic harps—I am now a professional Celtic harper—and sent me to Wales, to Aberdyfi and the gorgeous Tal-y-Llyn." (And with those words she was sending me right back to the places of my childhood, in longing.)

Most of us who have been on the children's book lists for a long time have correspondents like these: remote friends, keepers of our worldwide, timeless, imagination. These are the children too. Like the fourteen-year-old girl who wrote me just one remarkably self-aware letter perhaps fifteen years ago, and who has haunted me ever since. I often wonder what has become of her. "I just wanted to tell you how much your books have meant to me," she wrote. "They have helped me to see the good and evil in myself."

We must take loving care of those imaginations. Through their connection with our own, they are our stake in tomorrow. As Graham Greene said: "The books are always there, the moment of crisis waits, and now our children in their turn are taking down the future and opening the page."

Swords and Ploughshares

A talk for the Children's Literature New England institute, Swords
and Ploughshares, *Harvard University, August 1993*

War, the focus of this conference, is a brutal, bloody matter, and
we should never forget that. So I start by giving you two bloody
images, without apology.

My father was a young soldier in World War I, plunged, like so
many, into terror and bravado at the age of eighteen. In a break
between advances over the muddy, stinking battlefield that was
northern France in 1917, he found himself sheltering from gun-
fire in a shellhole with an older rifleman, a friend, who had had
enough.

"I'm going to get a Blighty, Jack," said the other soldier. Blighty
meant England, and a Blighty was the name for a small wound
just severe enough to get you shipped home.

"So he got up and showed himself over the edge," said my
father, on the single occasion I ever heard him tell this story,
"and a shell blew his head off. Pieces of it went all over me, and
the blood was like a burst pipe, spraying everywhere."

World War I was called "the war to end wars," and it killed a
large proportion of my father's generation: 900,000 from Britain
and what was then the Empire; 1,300,000 French, 1,750,000
Germans, and 116,000 Americans. It all added up to twice the

total of all the people killed in all wars from 1790 to 1913. God knows how much talent lost, how many potential leaders. The Treaty of Versailles which was supposed to tie up all the ends very soon began to unravel, and twenty-one years later, Europe exploded into an even more disastrous war.

My father and my surviving uncles were too old to fight in World War II, so they joined the ranks of the desperate citizens trying to put out fires and save lives during the bombing, as the cities burned. My Uncle Jimmy was a surgeon at a big London hospital where there was an endless delivery of casualties. The one image he could never get out of his mind was that of a little boy rescued from a bombed house, brought in on a stretcher, mute with shock. His head hadn't been blown off but it had been terribly damaged, and he lay there with one small hand up beside it, the fingers fiddling with what they found. Jimmy said, "He was playing with his own brains."

The little boy died. World War II killed more than 46 million men, women and children, 33 million of them in Europe. *Forty-six million people.* Nobody was killed by war inside the United States but 400,000 American troops died abroad. Inside Great Britain, which is about the size of Kansas, 60,000 civilians were killed during air raids, most of them in the first years, before Pearl Harbor put the United States into the war.

There are three ways in which wars involve children. Children as killers: the boys, and sometimes girls, in their teens, who are drafted to fight the wars. Children as victims, innocent, irrelevant, killed or maimed because they are in the way of a bullet or a bomb. And children as survivors, living in a country which is occupied by an enemy, or under physical attack—these children are undamaged, but because of their youth, altered. Those of us here who are over fifty probably come into that third category, especially if we were on the other side of the Atlantic during World War II.

I was four years old when the war began in Europe, and ten when it ended. The Jesuits say, I understand, give me a child until he is eight years old and I have him for life. I believe war has me for life, as a writer. Most people I know who have fought in a war never talk about it, because they have seen and done things they would rather try to forget. I have no such horrors to suppress, nor am I haunted by particular images, though to this day I jump at loud noises, and feel a split second of fear when a siren wails up-and-down with the sound the British air-raid siren made in World War II. But I know that the shape of my imagination, and all its unconscious preoccupations, were molded by my having been a child in war.

Most writers of my generation have done their war book, usually in middle age. I wrote mine earlier than most, when I was thirty-four. It is called *Dawn of Fear,* and it is an autobiographical story of a child's gradual discovery that war is not exciting and heroic, but terrible. Every word of it is a recording of events that actually happened, though a few are edited—for instance, I turned myself from a girl into a boy. I didn't need to change my two closest friends, since they were boys already. I don't quite know why I performed this sex change; it can't have had anything to do with the possible preferences of my child audience, since I thought I was writing an adult novel. We had better not examine it.

Westlands Avenue, Huntercombe, Buckinghamshire, was a small road twenty-three miles outside London. Along one end of it ran the main road to the West, and along the opposite end, on the other side of a field, was the main railway line. Once the war began, German bombers were always trying to hit the railway line, so the field between us and it was occupied by an anti-aircraft post, with soldiers and big impressive guns. Much to our disgust we could never get close to the guns; they were surrounded by an impenetrable fence.

I don't know that the anti-aircraft post did us much immediate good, since pretty soon the Germans seemed to be aiming bombs at it as well as at the railway line, but it did give us an early air-raid warning. The standard up-and-down wail that filled the air when the bombers were coming was broadcast across the countryside from, I think, the roof of the local police station, but the soldiers at the anti-aircraft post were alerted by telephone before

139

that. So whenever we heard their warning to each other, which was the hollow sound of someone rapping a metal bar on a pipe, we knew that in a few moments we would also hear, far louder, the awful first rising wail of the siren. Unless it happened to be four o'clock in the afternoon, in which case the pipe-rapping was just summoning the soldiers to have their tea. England is England, even when there's a war on.

The night raids were the worst. It wasn't a good thing to go to bed seeing a big moon in a clear sky, not if you'd ever overheard a grown-up saying apprehensively, looking up at it, "Bombers' moon . . ." But you would fall asleep, being a tired active child—to be woken by that siren, and anxious parents picking your little brother out of his cot, pulling you out of bed, wrapping a raincoat over your pyjamas. Out of the back door you go, scurrying to the air-raid shelter by the shaded light of a flashlight, though it's not pitch dark anyway, not with the moon, and the weaving arms of the searchlights crisscrossing the sky, and sometimes the bright bursts of explosions punctuating the drone of the planes.

The shelter was a big hole dug in the back lawn, lined and roofed with the rippled rectangles of galvanized iron that had arrived from the government, for families to make protective caves. The roof was covered with earth and grass so that the shelter looked like a round barrow; we were all three thousand years back in the Bronze Age. I liked it at first, being always enamored of small self-contained worlds. The shelter was a little square room, smelling of damp earth. You went down into it by steps sheltered with a wall of sandbags, and there were four bunks, on one of which I went to sleep, sometimes. Sometimes, but not often. There was too much noise. The guns hammered away at the end of the road, and the bombs came down with a whistle and a kind of *crump* sound that grew more thunderous, of course, the nearer they got. The earth shook, and so did the smoking flame of the single candle stuck to an old saucer, on the earth floor.

Our house was never hit; the bomb that came nearest fell six or seven houses away, just down the road. Once, a stick of bombs fell near our school, though we didn't know until next morning,

And I've remembered. But the sight was too big for me to comprehend, then. It was a much smaller incident which frightened me for the first time. Months later, when the siren went as usual and we scurried out into the night, the sound of planes was far louder and lower than it normally was. There were British fighters up there, intercepting the German bombers. I paused, looking up, hoping for one of the dogfights you sometimes saw between Spitfires and Messerschmitts in a blue daytime summer sky—and in the same moment a German plane came roaring low over the road with its guns blazing. My father yelled, "Get down!" and he knocked me down the steps into the shelter. When I burst into tears it wasn't because of the guns' violence but because of his: it took his fear for me to make me afraid.

Other things happened too, to make me afraid, but I don't need to describe them because they're on paper already in *Dawn of Fear*. Fear is my personal legacy of war. I've been fighting it all my life, often without success: fear of the dark, fear of deep water, fear of large gatherings of people. It's possible that I would have been a natural-born coward whatever the year of my birth, but I don't think being a child in wartime exactly helped.

It's really an unattached, almost abstract fear that I'm talking about. During the war I wasn't much frightened of specific things, even after the incident of the machine-gunning plane. The pattern of the air raids was so familiar that you simply learned to hope, or pray, that the killer bomb would miss your own head. This was true even later in the war, when the Germans began sending over V-1s, also known as buzz bombs or doodlebugs. The V-1s were fast, pilotless planes filled with explosives, sent off with just enough fuel in their tanks to reach the South of England, preferably the London area. They generally arrived in daytime, with no warning. You would hear the noisy, sputtering sound of the buzz bomb's engine, and then it would abruptly cut out, and there would be a nasty silence while it dived, perhaps toward you, perhaps not, and you simply had to wait for the explosion. (It would be a large explosion. A buzz bomb caused damage for a square quarter of a mile around.)

One of them came very close to us when I was nine years old, and there was the silence, and then a huge bang, and the window blew in. And I found myself giggling, there surrounded by bits of broken glass—because I was in the bathroom at the time, and during that tense ominous silence I'd thought only how *undignified* it was going to be, to be killed at last while sitting on the loo.

Real fear, for a child, didn't come at moments like that. It came at night. Not in the high-adrenaline nights when there were air raids. Nor in the first years of the Blitz, when our bedrooms were briefly occupied by bombed-out Londoners, and we all four slept in the living room, its windows barricaded with furniture to protect us from blast. But later, when I was back in my own bedroom, always when the light went out I *knew* there was a German paratrooper hiding in the wardrobe, or behind the door. I could hear him breathing. I could see his shadow move. He was waiting, he would come out any minute now, to kill us all. . . .

I am told sometimes that one of the most frightening moments in *The Dark Is Rising* is a scene in Will's bedroom at night, near the beginning of the book, when the Dark sends fear attacking him: a Feeling, that has something to do with snow and sinister rooks, but is really pure stark fear itself. If the scene is in fact effective, I owe it all to the illusory German paratrooper; to the war.

There *were* occasionally paratroopers, but none of them would have had much chance of making it to my wardrobe. Even when an English fighter pilot was forced to bale out over his own country after desperately fighting off German planes, he was liable to be greeted on landing by a fierce old lady with a pitchfork, or even to be shot at by the local Home Guard. My father was a sergeant in the Home Guard, a uniformed civil defense force for any male Englishmen who couldn't get into the services. His tin hat hung on the coat rack, his rifle stood in the umbrella stand, and we gazed at it with awe, strictly forbidden to touch it. Father went off regularly to go on duty, and had to be called out in emergencies by a runner, since we had no telephone. He did once have to lead his platoon in pursuit of a paratrooper, and was very nearly shot while circling a haystack, by one of his own men, who was circling it in the other direction *longing*, desperately, to kill a German.

My father had a great deal of pleasure, much later in life, watching a BBC television series which was full of the more far-cical antics of the Home Guard. *Dad's Army*, it was called. It was hilarious. Life does offer certain consolation prizes for the con-dition of war: one is heroism, another is humor. We were never short of heroes, when I was a child. They ranged from individual gallant soldiers, sailors or airman, especially fighter pilots flying Spitfires or Hurricanes, all the way up to Mr. Churchill. Winnie. We had a ferocious respect for him which didn't stop us from mimicking his famous exhortations about this being Our Finest Hour. (One of the nicest of the mock Churchill stories had him putting an aside into one of his most celebrated perorations: "We shall fight on the beaches, we shall fight on the landing grounds, we shall fight in the fields and in the streets, we shall beat the buggers about the heads with bottles, that's all we've got.")

People do laugh in wartime. They have to. We skipped in the playground to obscene rhymes about Germans, of which, unfor-tunately, the only one I can remember is very tame:

> Whistle while you work,
> Hitler is a twerp.

We saw cheery notices on the doors of shops whose windows had been blown out, saying things like "More open than usual." We listened to a splendid radio show called ITMA, acronym for *It's That Man Again*, in which a chirpy Everyman called Tommy Handley was surrounded by classic wartime characters. There was an indestructible Cockney charlady, Mrs. Mopp, who in spite of the most horrendous air raids would turn up with her bucket saying, "Can I do you now, sir?" Or there was Funf, the ineffectual German spy, who would telephone Handley and hiss in a thick adenoidal accent, "Dis is Funf spikking," and there

144

was Colonel Chinstrap and Signor So-so—oh, I could bore you for hours about ITMA, but I won't.

If the war bequeathed me fear, and a sense of the value of mockery, it also bequeathed me prejudice. I grew up hating Germans. Of course. They were the enemy. Jerry. The Hun. There was no such thing as a good German. Hitler was the Antichrist, and his minions came pretty close, fat Goering, little Goebbels, chilly Himmler and the rest. Tagging after them came Lord Haw Haw, an American-Irish-Briton who broadcast malevolent propaganda from Germany in a parody British accent, always beginning "Jairmany calling, Jairmany calling." He fell into the hands of the British after the war, and was tried and hanged as a traitor. It was unthinkable that a British subject could leave Britain, let alone help the Germans, who were trying to kill us all.

All this is almost fifty years past, but I've still never brought myself to visit Germany, and probably never shall. I dislike the sound of the language, and I can't listen to Wagner. Yes, I adore Mozart and Schubert, but they were *Austrian*. There's no escaping the fact that I'm biased. I can only take care that I remember it, and resist it—and wonder rather gloomily what will happen if my daughter announces one day that she's fallen in love with a German boy and is going to move to Hamburg. Of course, perhaps that would do me a lot of good.

Above all, war polarizes a child's view of the world. Everything becomes deceptively simple: there are the good guys, and the bad guys. Us, and Them. The good, and the evil. The enlightened, and the misguided. The Light, and the Dark.

I suppose there are plenty of reasons why I should have spent a large chunk of my life writing the five fantasy novels of the *Dark Is Rising* sequence, dealing with the struggle for control of the earth between the forces of good and of evil, the Light and the Dark. Fantasy is founded in myth, and one of the great themes of myth is the conflict between good and evil. And I was soaked in fairy tale and myth and folklore from the age of about three. Then there's religion. I was raised in the Church of England, drenched in liturgical music and marinated in the King James Bible, not to mention *Paradise Lost*, later on. And even though I turned away from Christianity when I was sixteen, you don't get rid of God and the Devil as easily as that. Their images lurk in your unconscious forever, like a watermark in paper.

Nevertheless, I think the deepest roots of my books are embedded in war. They are roots which go down down down to primitive man, if you follow them far enough. When *The Dark Is Rising* was first published, its identification of good as Light, and evil as Dark, was attacked by the Council for Inter-Racial Relations. But the metaphor has nothing to do with skin color, for goodness' sake. It's a very basic matter of day and night, from the time of the earliest human consciousness. Day is when the sun shines and warms you, and you can see what's coming. Night is dark and cold, and things can jump at you out of the darkness and eat you, particularly if you haven't yet discovered fire. Night is dangerous, and those lethal creatures attacking you are obviously bad.

Down in the air-raid shelter at the age of six, I was back with Cro-Magnon Man. Night was dangerous. Bad things happened in the dark. This was clearly the natural course of events, that there was a whole nation of people out there who wanted to kill us, and they came at night and dropped bombs. Our parents talked about a time called "Before the War," but that had no reality for me or my friends, we had no memory of it. Children are bound to think of their own surroundings as normal, having had no experience of anything else. This was reality, for us: the perilous dark, followed by the reassuring light of day.

The first time in our lives when we were allowed out into the dark to go somewhere other than to an air-raid shelter was the night of May 8, 1945. It was VE Day: Victory in Europe. There were bonfires in every neighborhood, with people singing, laughing, crying, out of relief. We walked along our street holding little flickering stubs of candle, safe in the darkness for the first time. We even saw a few fireworks: a tame display compared to the kinds of lights we were used to seeing in the sky, but incomparably better because they were not designed to kill.

But there was nothing cozy about the triumphing Light. Ultimately, the overwhelming image of my tenth year was that of the searing brilliance of the explosion of the atomic bomb which was dropped on Hiroshima three months later, on August 6, 1945. Though victory in Japan, like a large part of the war with Japan, seemed to us to belong largely to the Americans, this was the final victory of Our Side, sealed by the second bomb dropped on Nagasaki three days later. In the instant the Hiroshima bomb exploded, 80,000 people were killed; in the instant the Nagasaki bomb exploded, 40,000. The total, of 120,000, in two seconds, was precisely double the number of civilians killed in Britain during the whole six years of war. And of course it grew and grew, as more people died increasingly horrific deaths from radiation over the months and years.

And in this too my identification of the Dark and the Light has its roots. The adolescence of my generation was haunted by the memory of that brilliant light, and its mushroom cloud, just as our childhood had been noisy with more old-fashioned bombs.

In the third book of the *Dark Is Rising* sequence, *The Grey King*, there is an exchange between the Welsh shepherd John Rowlands, an ordinary man who is an observer and ultimately a kind of victim, and the boy who is an Old One of the Light, Will Stanton. John Rowlands says, "Those men who know anything at all about the Light also know that there is a fierceness to its power, like the bare sword of the law, or the white burning of the sun."

The book goes on:

Suddenly his voice sounded to Will very strong, and very Welsh. "At the very heart, that is. Other things, like humanity, and mercy, and charity, that most good men hold more precious than all else, they do not come first for the Light. Oh, sometimes they are there; often, indeed. But in the very long run the concern of you people is with the absolute good, ahead of all else. You are like fanatics. Your masters, at any rate. Like the old Crusaders—oh, like certain groups in every

147

belief, though this is not a matter of religion, of course. At the centre of the Light there is a cold white flame, just as at the centre of the Dark there is a great black pit bottomless as the Universe."

Will sighs—Will who is a representative of the Light—and he says, that's true, but you misjudge us because you are a man. "We are here," he says,

. . . simply to save the world from the Dark. Make no mistake, John, the Dark is rising, and will take the world to itself very soon if nothing stands in its way. And if that should happen, then there would be no question ever, for anyone, either of warm charity or of cold absolute good, because nothing would exist in the world or in the hearts of men except that bottomless black pit. The charity and the mercy and the humanitarianism, they are the only things by which men are able to exist together in peace. But in this hard case that we the Light are in, confronting the Dark, we can make no use of them. We are fighting a war. We are fighting for life or death—not for our life, remember, since we cannot die. For yours.

Then he says, "Sometimes, in this sort of a war, it is not possible to smooth the way for one human being, because even that one small thing could mean an end of the world for all the rest." And John Rowlands says, "It is a cold world you live in, *bachgen*. I do not think so far ahead, myself. I would take the one human being over the principle, all the time."

So would I. But that is my adolescence talking, not my childhood. That cold white flame at the heart of the Light, and Will's justification of it, come from the absolute certainty I was given, when I was small, that *we were right*. Hitler was evil, and the greedy advance of the Third Reich across Europe was the rising of the Dark. Little Britain, Jack the Giant-Killer, was the last repository of the Light, and anything we did to defeat the Dark was okay. Even our churches confirmed this: one should pray for victory, said the Archbishop of Canterbury, adding to the prayer "if it be thy will" or "for the victory of righteousness."

There was one bishop in the Church of England during World War II, George Bell, Bishop of Chichester, who attacked Britain's retaliatory night-bombing of German cities, with its inevitable killing of civilians, as "a degradation of the spirit for all who take part in it." He demanded, in the House of Lords, "How can the War Cabinet fail to see that this progressive devastation of cities is threatening the roots of civilization?" But this was such an unpopular view that when a Battle of Britain commemoration service was held at the Bishop's own cathedral in 1943, his dean had to ask him not to preach.

The self-righteousness of the Light is no doubt preferable to the depravity of the Dark, but it too holds great dangers. It can reach the point of a holy war, fought for the promotion of one of the historically militant religions, like Christianity or Islam—and at that point the Light enters the Dark, or vice versa, and gives birth to monstrosities like the Inquisition, or the death sentence pronounced on Salman Rushdie.

I'm with John Rowlands. I would take the one human being over the principle, all the time.

There will never be another war on the scale of World War II, because we should not survive it for five minutes. But I do not believe it is possible, or proper, to say to a child today, "One day there will be no more war, ever." It's not true. We belong to a flawed race. At this very moment, wars are being fought in scores of different places all over the globe. Human conflict is like a chronic forest fire, always flaring up in one place or another, because deep down, the layer of peat out of which the whole forest grows, the complex of human emotions, is burning.

Nor can you even say easily to a child, looking at one of these present wars, "Here is the bad side and here is the good." If that had been possible in the contentious Balkans which were briefly Yugoslavia, the blood-soaked chaos there could have been prevented before it began. In human life, the lines between "good" and "bad" tend to blur. Alongside my unconscious inheritance from World War II, I have a conscious conviction that we of the Light did even more damage to the Dark side than they had done to us. Against their Blitz, and the systematic horrors of the concentration camps and forced marches, you have to set our firebombing and carpet bombing of enemy cities, and the monstrosity of Fat Man and Little Boy, the two atomic bombs. In war, the Dark and the Light inevitably behave very much alike. That's why in *Silver on the Tree*, the last book of the *Dark Is Rising* series, the host of riders of the attacking Dark are robed not only in black but in white. Absolutes, whether they serve good or evil, are doomed to be always destructive, always cruel.

That's what books about war can say to children. That in the long run, the important thing is not absolute good, an implacable ideal, but the individual conscience of an imperfect human being. We are not Old Ones, creatures of the Light; each of us is a mortal mixture of the Light and the Dark. Children know this. Along the short road from the cradle, they have already made a lot of unpleasant discoveries: about the bully in the playground; about gangs and victims; about rage and pain, greed and revenge. A book which deals with war can illumine a lot of things they already know, so long as it is not a simplistic unrealistic portrait of faultless heroes vanquishing total snarling evil. (There is a place for stories like that, but they have to do with myth, not war.)

Mine is not a Christian viewpoint, along the militant Christ-focused lines of C. S. Lewis's *Narnia* books. As a matter of fact, earlier this year the *Dark Is Rising* books were accused by the Church of Scotland's Board of Social Responsibility of undermining the Christian faith. I think this is something of an overreaction (it's also twenty-one years late) but it's certainly true that you won't find a theistic ideal infusing those books. Instead there is the echo of the author, the wartime child and postwar adolescent, observing conflict and imperfection. Looking back at the books now, I can hear this most of all in the long speech which is Merriman's farewell to the children who have struggled to help the cause of the Light.

"Remember," he says,

. . . that it is altogether your world now. You and all the rest. We have delivered you from evil, but the evil that is inside men is at the last a matter for men to control. The responsibility and the hope and the promise are in your hands—your hands and the hands of the children of all men on this earth. The future cannot blame the present, just as the present cannot blame the past. The hope is always here, always alive, but only your fierce caring can fan it into a fire to warm the world.

Then for a moment he becomes very English, quoting a legend not much known outside England: that Sir Francis Drake, admiral of the first Queen Elizabeth, who saved Britain from the Spanish Armada in the sixteenth century, lies sleeping in his hammock under the ocean, waiting for the day when England will need him to come back and save her again. It was a legend remembered quite often at tense moments during World War II. Merriman says,

For Drake is no longer in his hammock, children, nor is Arthur somewhere sleeping, and you may not lie idly expecting the second coming of anybody now, because the world is yours and it is up to you. Now especially since man has the strength to destroy this world, it is the responsibility of man to keep it alive, in all its beauty and marvellous joy. . . .

. . . And the world will still be imperfect, because men are imperfect. Good men will still be killed by bad, or sometimes by other good men, and there will still be pain and disease and famine, anger and hate. But if you work and care and are watchful, as we have tried to be for you, then in the long run the worse will never, ever, triumph over the better. And the gifts put into some men, that shine as bright as Eirias the sword, shall light the dark corners of life for all the rest, in so brave a world.

Books about war can be valuable for children, pointing the way from swords to ploughshares. But they can do it only by saying to them, "This doesn't *have* to happen again. It's up to you."

A Plea for the Book

A talk for the 11th Annual Authors Symposium at the University of
Arkansas, Little Rock, October 1993

If you look at the flyer which describes the authors at this sym-
posium, you will go down the list and find it telling you that
Nonny Hogrogian is a native New Yorker, that David Kherdian is
from Racine, Wisconsin, that Peter Catalanotto grew up in East
Northport, Long Island. Then the list gets to me, and it takes on
a distinct air of reproach. It says, "Susan Cooper has lived in the
United States for over three decades *without becoming an
American.*"

How could she do that?

It's true, I'm afraid. Since dual citizenship isn't available to me
I'm a permanent resident alien, carrying what used to be known
as a green card. I do consider myself a sort of honorary
American, after having lived and worked here for so long, and
paid my taxes, and produced two firmly American children. But
there is one sense in which I am decidedly un-American, and so
is every person in this room. It is not an American activity to be
attending a symposium which is all about books. The culture
which we have allowed to evolve in this country, and which we
are passing on to our children, is not friendly to the book, or
even to the word. In the United States today we have the culture

of the image; we are living in the Age of the Screen. It is infinitely seductive and powerful, and terribly dangerous.

The extent of that danger has really been brought home to us this year by the government report *Adult Literacy in America*, which the U.S. Secretary of Education Richard Riley called "a wake-up call to the sheer magnitude of illiteracy in this country." At the heart of the 150-page forest of statistics in this report is the simple shattering revelation that some 90 million adult Americans are either illiterate or sadly inept at reading, writing and comprehension.

These 90 million can't write a letter explaining that an error has been made in a bill. They can't read an article and afterwards answer questions on its content, or explain its argument. They are not at home with their own language—though they think they are, which is even more frightening. Although they may skim a newspaper or a magazine from time to time, it's unlikely that they ever choose to read a book. This is 47 percent of the population we are talking about: almost half the total of people aged sixteen and over, walking about out there. And unless our schools are about to undergo a huge instant rise in standards, it's a fair bet that 47 percent of the children now in school may end up the same way.

Now it's easy to snipe at this report, which was largely carried out by the Educational Testing Service, who also conduct the SATs and all their inflexible multiple-choice siblings. How can they be sure that the 26,000 people they surveyed truly represent an adult population of 191 million? What about the 32 million Americans whose first language is something other than English? Maybe that figure slants the statistics; maybe the findings tell us not about literacy but about poverty, discrimination, the breakdown of the family: about the victims of a society whose highest value is the acquisition of wealth.

Maybe, indeed. But that makes no difference to the importance of this survey to people like you and me: people whose lives are so closely involved with books, and children. We can't afford to ignore it, or to argue with its findings. I'm not suggesting that books are an endangered species. Far from it. There are more of them around than there ever have been—some 90,000 are published in the U.S.A. every year. Too many, in fact, just as there are too many kinds of breakfast cereal—and for the same depressing commercial reasons. Children's books are one of the most lucrative parts of the publishing industry.

But the children don't seem to be reading with any more frequency or competence than the adults. Almost 40 percent of American schoolchildren never read a novel outside their schoolwork, or read just one a year. Only 27 percent spend any time reading a book every day, for pleasure. Think about those figures. And then consider a sourceless quotation which has reverberated in my head for decades: "It is what you read when you don't have to, that determines what you will be when you can't help it."

Once upon a time, when I was a child, books had all our attention. There was no competition. This was Britain, where the economy was in ruins for almost a decade after World War II, and so no television set appeared in our house until I was about fifteen years old. There was radio, of course, and we loved it— but then radio, that lovely medium, consists either of music or of the written word read aloud. And radios weren't as portable then as books.

My earliest memory is of being given a book. It is in fact a faintly shameful memory, because it goes back to the day my mother brought my baby brother home for the first time, from the hospital. I was three and a half years old. I haven't the least memory of seeing my baby brother, but I remember crystal clear the enormous anthology of nursery rhymes, drawings and small stories which my mother brought home at the same time. She gave me it with her first greeting hug. It was almost too large for me to hold, and I sat down with it instantly and wasn't heard from for hours.

My mother was a very clever woman. She knew her daughter. In one stroke, with that book, she not only destroyed sibling rivalry but she began my literary education. By the time my brother was weaned, she told me later, I had taught myself to read.

A great deal later, I produced my own two children, Jonathan and Kate, eighteen months apart. When I brought Jonathan's new baby sister home to meet him, he was only eighteen months old, so he could hardly retreat into literacy. But whenever I was breast-feeding Kate, Jon would somehow manage to come trotting into the room carrying a book—any book. He would push the book onto my lap, pointedly ignoring the hungry baby glued to my bosom, and say with heart-rending insistence, "Read to me, Mummy!" I suppose I had a very clever son, who knew his mother; clearly my family has cyclical genes. So of course I did read to him, and perhaps Kate was listening as well, between burps, because both of them were doing their own reading by the time they were four. The teacher at their nursery school was very distressed when she found I was encouraging them to read. "Oh, not so soon!" she said. "You should let them enjoy their childhood!" She had a sweet nature, but she was a very silly woman.

In the defense of books, there is no stronger weapon than giving children the chance to learn to read when they are very, very young. Far more of them want to learn than you might think— to achieve that marvelous freedom. It's the next great magic after learning to walk and talk. Think of that first realization, that we have all forgotten. You are a child who loves to hear stories, but you can't hear them unless the storyteller is around and willing to tell you one—and then you discover that through these marks on paper, you can, if you try, hear a story in your own head whenever you want one. The story doesn't belong just to this powerful person who's reading it to you; it's available, in those marks, those words, on the pages of a book.

I firmly believe that one of the things that turned me into a writer was the matter of being surrounded, very early in life, by written words: the feeling that they were important, the awareness of their magical properties. I love words, as a painter loves colors, as a composer loves sound, as a gardener loves putting seeds in the earth. We all do, those of us who make books, or stories, or poems. Obviously an early awareness of books isn't the only thing that makes someone a writer; you also have to be lucky enough to be born with the right talent and imagination and obsession. But it all has to begin with the reading. If you are concerned for the future of our civilization, there is no more cheering sight than a boy or girl who is lost in a book. It's an image I cling to, in moments of depression: the absorbed child, reading. If he—or she—is reading one of my books, he's accepting a gift, and justifying my existence. Like every other children's author, I have offered him my imagination. "I have spread my dreams under your feet," said Aedh, in Yeats's poem. "Tread softly, because you tread on my dreams." The child who opens and enters the book is treading softly; he links his own imagination to mine, and the private world in which I wrote becomes his own private world, while he reads.

Wonderful loyalties can be forged in this way, and sometimes they outlast childhood. There's a story related to this that I always wanted to tell the English author Richmal Crompton—though I can't now, because she's dead. It's about my own two children, Jonathan and Kate, the pair who liked to read.

Instead of spending holidays on Cape Cod like most normal people in Massachusetts, my husband and I had built a little holiday house on a remote island in the Caribbean, one of the British Virgin Islands, and this was where we and the children spent our holidays. (I was married to a professor, so we had those long academic summers.) Arriving in this Paradise, you would expect two children cramped from a long journey to go instantly leaping over the golden beach and jump into the warm blue sea. Not a bit of it. Not yet. Instead, like thirsty travelers in a desert, Kate and Jon would rush through the house to their bedroom, and fling themselves on the box where their books were stored. Their island books, accumulated over the years from the one bookshop in the British Virgin Islands; dozens of books which were old friends whom they hadn't seen since last year. Kate specially loved Joan Aiken's books, Jonathan was particularly attached to a book called *Just William* by Richmal Crompton, and all its sequels, dealing with a wonderfully eccentric English schoolboy called, of course, William. They would pull the books joyfully out of the box, and there they would lie on their beds, these two, reading, while the sun shone outside unnoticed over the Caribbean Sea.

Jump ahead fifteen years. The children grow up. Things change. Three years ago Hurricane Hugo hit the Virgin Islands, and wrecked our house. I went down to check the damage, and standing rather tearfully in a roomful of rubble, I found that the telephone still worked. So I called my son, at the University of Florida, where he was a graduate student.

"It's terrible," I said, "the roof's blown off, and the walls have collapsed, and the kitchen's full of water—" and I went on with this litany of disaster, for a long time.

Jon was twenty-four years old by then, a big tough engineer, six feet three, an oarsman who'd been stroke of the Cornell University eight. When I finished my tale of woe, there was a small silence at the other end of the phone, and then he said, "Mom, I know it's kind of a weird question, but are my William books all right?"

That's what I wish I could have told Richmal Crompton.

With stories like this it's quite possible to lull oneself into a sense of false security about books and reading and the young. The generation of the baby boomers has grown up into yuppiehood, and they have all begun to buy books for their own children. Fifteen years ago it was rare to find a children's bookshop in the United States, but today there are more than 350. Book clubs sell paperbacks—and videos and other spin-offs, but mostly books—through the schools, to children of whom four-fifths, they say, would be unlikely ever to set foot in a bookshop. And though public and school libraries had their funding severely cut during both the Reagan and Bush administrations, to a point where they make up not 80 percent of the children's book market but 60 percent—in spite of that, the total number of books sold has not dropped. It's gone up. Someone is buying all those books. The question is, are the children reading them?

Two years ago the *Christian Science Monitor* published a poll of 2,200 children aged from five to nineteen, all over the U.S.A. Many of the teenagers said they didn't read books, ever, "because they are boring." A boy in Wisconsin said, "I don't read, I watch TV, because TV is more interesting and it doesn't take as long." (This reminds me of an English girl, aged sixteen, who recently had lunch with a friend of mine in New York. "You must have read Susan Cooper's books," said my loyal friend. "Oh, you mean *The Dark Is Rising,*" said the girl. "No, I never read that. It was too thick.")

The *Monitor* survey asked the children what proportion of their spare time they spent reading, as against watching television. They said, 28 percent reading, 67 percent watching TV. Which did they *like* better? Reading 39 percent, TV 58 percent—a 10 percent switch in the other direction. How's that again? They prefer reading, but they don't do it? One fifteen-year-old from Utah said, "For every hour I watch TV, I probably spend three to five minutes reading. The weird thing is, I *like* reading books."

It's not weird. Not if you take seriously, as few people do, the fact that television, like alcohol, is a drug. It is easier to turn that little screen on than to turn it off. People of any age who are addicted to it tend to reach for the control knob as soon as they walk through the door. It's not hard to find the knob: according to *The New York Times*, 94.2 percent of all American homes have a television set—and of those, 70 percent have two sets and 34 percent have three. Another recent survey reported that 71 percent of American thirteen-year-olds watch three or more hours of television a day. *Every day, including schooldays.* And yet another, surveying younger children, found that children between the ages of two and eleven in this country watch an average of 28 hours of television every week. Twenty-eight hours a week means *four* hours a day, every day. Four hours of that empty hypnotized expression that you see on the faces of kids watching some mindless quiz show, or comedy series with fake laugh track. Nine-tenths of the stuff they watch isn't doing a thing for them; it isn't reaching anything but the surface of their minds, and when it's over they will forget most of it instantly. And the imagination that could have been involved, stretched, developed, dwindles away just a little bit more, like a muscle losing its strength because it isn't used.

Hollywood, as the screenwriter Larry Gelbart says, "has chosen to transform itself into a software factory whose product is designed to make a relatively few wealthy, while impoverishing our culture to a devastating degree." And one of the television critics of *The New York Times*, Walter Goodman, says just as uncompromisingly, "The fact that so many children spend four or more hours a day in front of a television set helps explain why ignorance is rampant."

That ignorance is what the former Librarian of Congress Daniel Boorstin once called "the price tag that history has placed on our civilization." Our commercially directed pop culture, fed by advertising, is, alas, America's most powerful gift to the planet. There are Coke signs in China, and McDonald's in Moscow, and blue jeans everywhere, and they all come out of a society in which we don't have people, we have consumers. Our culture is based on the idea of seizing the imagination for one specific purpose— to drive its owner to buy something. It could be said that you put your child's imagination at risk every time you open a newspaper, turn on any television channel other than PBS, drive past the billboards on a city street, or walk through a supermarket. As for the average child and his four hours of television a day—I shudder to think how many craftily made commercials he or she will sit through. And if Mother drags him away from the television set to accompany her to the supermarket, she will find all the most sugary, candylike, television-advertised breakfast cereals set out carefully on the lowest shelves of the aisle—at her child's eye level.

This is the richest country in the world. But among the 155 member countries of the United Nations, the United States ranks not first but 49th in its level of literacy. And its status isn't rising. In the past twenty years, according to the president of the American Federation of Teachers, there has been a huge drop in American children's verbal SAT scores: 116,000 scored above 600 in 1972, but only 75,000 in 1992, even though there were more children taking the test. And nationwide, 30 percent of this year's freshmen starting college will need remedial reading classes. In 1990 the National Governors Association, including then-Governor Clinton, set six educational goals, of which one stated: "By the year 2000, every adult American will be literate." This was echoed in the National Literacy Act passed by Congress the following year. But it's not going to happen. Eighty percent of the people who will make up the workforce in the year 2000 are already-employed adults, and if we're to believe that new government report, almost half of them have a literacy problem and don't even know it.

There are thousands, millions, of people out there like, for instance, Lawrence Williams of Alexandria, Louisiana, who worked quite happily for years cleaning his cotton-cutting machine by hand, until the day when the blades slipped gear and his left arm was severed above the elbow. There was a printed notice beside the factory machine warning "Always clean with a stick, never by hand," but Mr. Williams couldn't read, and nor could the older man who'd taught him his job when he started. When he was asked how he'd managed to graduate from high school, Mr. Williams said, "They gave me Cs just for showing up. When I tried to do anything I'd get Fs."

The National Workplace Literacy Program, created in 1985, has invested $41 million in grants for adult literacy training, but still only 15,000 companies across the country have formal programs to teach their employees to read properly. That's half of 1 percent of the 3.8 million companies in the U.S.A. And in the meantime overcrowded, understaffed high schools are still pumping out the time-honored proportion of graduates like Lawrence Williams. There aren't just cracks in our system, there are great gaping holes.

I grew up in the British educational system, of course. It's changed since then, but not radically. In this country I've shepherded two children through public school and two through private school, not to mention universities and graduate schools. That's only four children, so I'm no expert—and I'm certainly not qualified to talk about the way English is taught in every American classroom. But I do know that while my kids and stepkids were growing up, at every educational level, in every subject, I found less stress on language, and more on things like multiple-choice testing, in American schools than in British. It's one reason why Britain's problems with illiteracy or semiliteracy, though much bewailed over there, seem ludicrously small when you look at them from here.

On a world scale, consider some large facts. First fact: English is the first language for more people on this planet than any other language except Mandarin Chinese. As a second language it beats even Mandarin, and heads the list. Altogether it's spoken by 770 million people. Second fact: without language we cannot communicate. The more accurate our use of language, the better our communication, and the better our chance of developing intelligent thought processes, which lead to intelligent decisions. Third fact: language requires words, and the proper use of words. Even on those television screens, actors and newsreaders and entertainers are speaking the language, using words.

And as for the world of computers, it is full of happy homes for the written word, from e-mail to the further boundaries of CD-ROM. In *The New York Times* recently, Paul Saffo, who's a fellow of the Institute of the Future (in California, of course) confirmed this by quoting Horace, which was rather a surprise. *Litera scripta manet*: The written word remains. "We talk endlessly about new tech-arcana like video and virtual reality," said Mr. Saffo, "but the conversation orbits round the stuff of this page—text. In fact the written word doesn't just remain; it is flourishing like kudzu vines at the boundaries of the digital revolution." In other words, the twenty-first-century computer will require the same old verbal skills as the pencil.

All these are the practical reasons why we must be able to use our language. Far beyond them goes the beauty of it, and the poetry that is in its prose. And all those young imaginations, which can never fully develop without the word and the page and the book.

So what can we do to improve matters?

Well, for starters I think it's cheering that we no longer have a man in the White House who uses the language like a salt-shaker. Here is a verbatim extract from an interview with former President Bush on C-Span in 1991.

> Watch quite a bit. I watch the news and I don't like to tell you this because you'll think I'm into some weird TV freak here, but we—I have a set that has five screens on it and I can sit on my desk and whip—just punch a button if I see one off on the corner, that moves into the middle screen, the other one goes to the side. Then I can run up and down the—up and down the dial. So I—and you can record all four—four going at once, while you—when you're watching, I don't quite know how to do that yet. But I cite this because Barbara accused me of being too much—not too much but plugged into TV too often, put it that way.

That's English?

President Clinton, on the other hand, is not only literate but articulate; he speaks, and writes, good English. I may be a trifle biased by the fact that we both spent some time at the same university, the place where the *Oxford English Dictionary* was born—but even so, it's undeniable that role models are important. Children are likely to notice, without perhaps being aware of it, that their Chief Executive not only wears a baseball cap and goes jogging but speaks in whole sentences, sometimes even using long words.

The best and most immediate role models in this respect are, of course, teachers and librarians. Their status in this culture of ours is far too low; so are their salaries, so are the amounts spent on their libraries and schools. Yet nobody, perhaps not even parents, is more powerful in the matter of bringing children to books. Those of us who write or illustrate children's books know this best of all.

Consider, for instance, part of a letter from a librarian who talked a teacher into doing a major project with his class on my fantasy novel *The Dark Is Rising,* the second book in a five-book sequence by the same name. This letter happened to come from England, but it's much like others I've had from the United States—I quote it because it's the most vivid. The librarian wrote:

> The class is in a school on a large postwar housing estate, of mixed ability and with an unsettled history. Their teacher was new at the school and undertook the reading of the book with them with some misgiving, but on my recommendation. . . . What pleased and surprised everyone was the way *The Dark Is Rising* became *their* book to that class, and their sheer enjoyment and enthusiasm spilled over into so many other things that they were doing in the class, in the school and at home.

She went on about the various things the children did as a result, making pictures and slides and posters, writing poems and recording them to jazz on cassettes, and spawning book clubs in other parts of the school. Then she said something I love: "For my part, I was closely questioned about the book and the author by the children when I went to see them, and after telling them about the other books in the series and leaving them a copy of *Greenwitch,* I had one of the greatest compliments a librarian can have—seeing a hand reach out surreptitiously and take the book from the pile before I had finished speaking."

I had letters from the children too, and my favorites came from two boys called Julian and Alan. Julian wrote: "Our teacher has now finished reading your book to us and I want to read your next book on my own. I thought it was a good idea that you put the light and the dark against each other. A good percentage of our class wanted the light to win, but the odd few wanted the dark to win—but they are the ones who are usually in trouble."

And Alan wrote, "I enjoyed *The Dark Is Rising* so much that I bought a paperback of it, and now my dad is halfway through it. It is a shame that it was not the last in the series because I wanted to know what happened at the end. About two weeks ago Miss Payne our librarian came and talked about your books, and she brought a copy of *Greenwitch,* and Perry Wilson, a boy in my class, beat me to read it."

That was the hand that reached out, I suppose. Good for Perry Wilson, good for Miss Payne. All the Miss Paynes, and the Mr. Paynes. That's an example of the way one librarian and one teacher can communicate enthusiasm—the kind of enthusiasm that sent them into librarianship or teaching in the first place, instead of into advertising or public relations or one of the other mainstays of our pop culture. They teach by using real books, not simply workbooks. They reach out to a bunch of average kids and say, "Hey—try this. You might like it."

But the schools and the libraries can't cope alone. We shall have children who can properly read and write only if we all become involved. It starts with parents, reading to their children—this should be a loving obligation for every parent who's even halfway literate. And an even greater responsibility for parents rests in the small matter of pressing a switch. I don't think *all* those children watching four hours of television every day are in the house on their own.

Last year, schools and librarians all over the country took part in the Children's Book Council's year-long initiative called Read Across America. Amongst the public figures who joined its honorary committee to make the cause more visible—speaking of role models—was Hillary Rodham Clinton. It would be cheering if that fact had some significance for the future; if both Clintons could turn some of the passion and energy they have devoted to the vital cause of health care to the equally vital cause of education. Here and there, good things are happening. Some of them are really exciting, like one which has been growing in New York City: an enterprise whose seeds we might be able to sow in your city, my city, all over the place. Eighteen months ago the publishing house of Bantam Doubleday Dell was moving to a new building, and they wanted to dispose usefully of thousands of books. They thought they might give them to underprivileged city schools, of which New York has many. So they went to the mayor's office, where they found that Joyce Dinkins, the mayor's wife, had a program called Reading for Recreation. Every so often she would bring a hundred first graders from some particularly disastrous school to visit Gracie Mansion, where she and visiting authors would read to them, give them juice and cookies and send them home with a book each. The whole thing had been funded with a grant of $10,000 from Planters Peanuts. The publishers were encouraged by this. They asked for advice. Craig Virden, of Bantam Doubleday Dell Books for Young People, says, "We thought we'd give a thousand books to a school in each of the five New York boroughs. And send volunteers in to help—to read to the kids, do anything. So the mayor's office chose the schools for us, five of the ones that were most at risk, based on raw reading scores, and we went in.

"I worked in a school in Brooklyn," said Mr. Virden. "It had a hundred percent turnover rate. What with shelters and all, there wasn't a single kid stayed in the same school for a year. They hadn't had a librarian for years, so we brought in new books, washed old ones, repaired shelves, read to the kids, refurbished the whole library. The faculty and administration were so delighted to find someone paying attention, they were overwhelmed. And using us as an example, the principal went out and got money from other companies, to help the school."

That last sentence is very important. Good example is a powerful thing. It's like that incident a few years ago when a philanthropic rich man adopted a whole class in a Harlem school and guaranteed to send them to college if they wanted to go—and within months there were a dozen rich people elsewhere doing the same. The publishers' Adopt-A-School program has grown, with four or five publishing houses helping about twenty schools in New York City. But it doesn't have to be limited to publishing houses. Any company can invest some money, and some of its employees' time, in encouraging local children to read; any company can adopt a school. You might even say that any company that's in profit has an obligation to do that, to give something back. Particularly companies whose profits depend to any degree on children as a market: television companies, people who make toys or sneakers or breakfast cereals. And what an investment in the future! Beyond that, every one of us should do what we can to increase that pathetic total—one half of 1 percent—of businesses who have remedial reading programs for adult employees, to teach nonliterate people to read. And even more, to encourage them to help the schools produce literate children in the first place. It's time for the aggressive, materialistic culture that has devalued reading, and all other gentle, contemplative pursuits, to come to the rescue of the language before it's too late. Remember that quotation? "It is what you read when you don't have to, that determines who you will be when you can't help it."

We're fighting a battle, those of us involved in the world of children's books: a lot of little guerrilla skirmishes, in the underground war to preserve the imagination. The Age of the Screen isn't going to go away; indeed it offers all kinds of wonderful possibilities, if it could just acquire a little more quality control. But there is one truth, one necessary dictum, that we must never forget: *Every child should be encouraged to read books, words on a page, for his or her own pleasure, in his own time, dreaming his own—and the author's—dream.* There is no substitute. None.

And when December is approaching, try whispering in the ear of any friend you have who's likely to go shopping for a child or a grandchild, a nephew or a niece. Say to them, "Psst! For every toy you buy for a child this Christmas—for every single toy, or video, or computer game—buy him or her a paperback book as well." In this noisy commercial world of ours, where the sunlight that nurtures the imagination has to filter down past the great looming skyscrapers of the computer and the television set, books need all the help they can get.

THE ALPHABET PEDLAR

A talk for the Children's Literature New England institute, "Image and Word: Patterns of Creativity," Mount Holyoke College, 1994

There was a time when meadow, grove and stream,
The earth, and every common sight,
To me did seem
Apparall'd in celestial light,
The glory and the freshness of a dream.
It is not now as it hath been of yore;—
Turn wheresoe'er I may,
By night or day,
The things which I have seen I now can see no more . . .

Thus William Wordsworth: sometimes a dreadful poet, sometimes quite marvelous. He was always obsessed, like Blake, with the awful inevitable erosion of the spirit that takes place when an innocent child sets forth on the lifetime journey through our difficult world.

Among my friends, especially those of my children's generation, I seem to have a singular number of people who work with very young children, either in libraries or kindergartens. And when they talk about their jobs, they all sound just like Wordsworth. They love what they do because they are exhilarated by the freshness and originality of the children they work with. They often call it creativity. They also sound very much like the bubbling letters I used to send across the Atlantic to my mother when my children were young: "You won't believe what Katie said today . . . You'll never guess what Jonnie did . . ."

Very young children are indeed quite wonderful, of course. In their discovery of the world we rediscover our own unfulfilled potential; in their startling early accomplishments we see the possibility that somewhere out there, toddling along, there may be a new Mozart, a new Shakespeare, a new Einstein. My friends who work with the very young are fueled by this excitement. But once in a while, in a reflective moment, every one of them says mournfully, just like Wordsworth, just like Blake, "Where does it go? What is it that stifles the freshness in these kids? What's wrong with our educational system? With our parents? With our culture?"

Well, there are certainly things wrong, with all of those, but I don't know that they're the villains. If you are faced every day with the glory and the freshness of the dream, perhaps it's hard to accept the fact that a child's amazingly original picture, or poem, or tune, or turn of phrase may actually owe more to the condition of youth than to a lasting "creativity." (I feel I should give this word quotation marks at least once, since my *Oxford English Dictionary* doesn't admit its existence.) Like everything else in this world, creativity is altered by time. Over the piano in my living room there is a framed picture in pastels, a sort of flowery abstract, which was done by my daughter when she was five. It hangs there because I like looking at it—as a picture, not as five-year-old Kate's picture. But I didn't necessarily expect Kate to go on drawing pictures, and indeed she didn't, she gradually gave it up, just as she gave up playing the piano and subsequently playing the flute. Instead she read a great many books, took up rowing, and did an honors degree in Russian. She changed. She grew up. The creativity didn't go away, mind you. It was absorbed, into the imagination. Kate's twenty-five now, she's working in children's book production at Little, Brown, in Boston, and loving it. The eye that looks critically at her color proofs is the eye of the five-year-old who painted that picture.

Creativity can certainly be nurtured, and obviously should be, but I don't think I believe it can be destroyed. Not at any rate the creativity of the artist, otherwise known as talent. Talent can be destroyed, or wasted, only by its owner. The regretful words of Wordsworth and Blake and my teacher friends are really directed not at the death of talent or creativity but at the corruption of innocence by experience. They're mourning the fact that we have to grow up; that the frolicking kitten has to become a mean, feisty cat, or for that matter a fat, somnolent cat. Changed. Talent, the means for what Tolkien called the Sub-Creative Art, is not affected by change. You can use it or waste it, but like perfect pitch, it does not go away; it is a genetic accident. A gift and a responsibility. I believe that as profoundly as I believe anything, and I put it into a book called *The Dark Is Rising*, twenty years ago. The archetypal wise old man Merriman is talking to eleven-year-old Will Stanton, who has just come into his inheritance as an Old One and finds it dismaying.

> "It is a burden," Merriman said. "Make no mistake about that. Any great gift or power or talent is a burden, and this more than any, and you will often long to be free of it. But there is nothing to be done. If you were born with the gift, then you must serve it, and nothing in this world or out of it may stand in the way of that service, because that is why you were born and that is the Law."

I shouldn't put it quite so portentously as that if I were talking to a young writer about her—or his—talent for writing, and I shouldn't leave out mention of the joy of work, but I'd say much the same thing. Katherine Paterson, discussing what she called the "sweat theory of good writing," once said, "We writers are not a breed apart, a privileged aristocracy doling out gifts to less fortunate mortals. . . . we are, like the majority of the human race, day laborers." This is absolutely true. However, it would be ludicrous to tell you that if you were just to labor hard enough, you would be able to write as well as Katherine Paterson. You wouldn't. Not without her talent. You must work like a dog to serve the gift, but first of all you have to be born with it.

It's a pity to confuse the boniness of talent with the bloom of youth, by lumping them both together under the label of creativity. In her introduction to this institute, Barbara Harrison quoted Robert Coles's report on a girl named Doris, who was immensely creative when small, but by the time she was thirteen had stopped all her artwork and instead was making grimly practical comments about math and spelling and college entrance. I got the feeling Mr. Coles felt she'd been stifled—by her teachers, by the system. But who knows? Maybe thirteen-year-old Doris, like my Kate, gave up painting pictures not because society deadened her creative impulse but because she wasn't born to be a painter. That's all right. Not every choirboy grows up to be a concert baritone, but I wouldn't mind betting that in spite of that, most choirboys go on enjoying music all their lives. It's not the end of the world if Doris stopped making things—so long as she went on looking and seeing, listening and hearing, and reading and reflecting. So long as those early creative years gave her an active imagination.

This is the vital thing. The lively years, the time of discovery and delight and the unjaded eye—those are the years when a child's sponge-like imagination absorbs pictures and stories and images that will affect him or her, consciously or unconsciously, for the rest of life. If we encourage the originality, the freshness and the enjoyment, we have a better chance of raising tomorrow's audiences, tomorrow's readers, as well as tomorrow's artists. Those are the years for laying down really good compost. Every writer who's also a gardener comes up with this image sooner or later as a way of describing the imagination: it's a compost bed, in which myth and image and story ferment in order to feed the crop to come.

Writers, teachers, librarians, artists, parents, we are all respon-
sible for the nurturing of the imagination. Anything that lodged
in our own imagination, and put down roots and blossomed
there like a flowering tree—we can take the seed of that same
image and sow it in the imagination of a child, there to blossom
in the same way. If we're lucky. And if we're given help. Every so
often among my letters from children there will be one that says,
"I never liked fantasy before, but Miss Shapiro gave me one of
your books to read and then I went off and read the whole series
and please will you write another?" And I think with warmth of
this teacher or librarian, who liked a book and planted a seed in
the fertile soil of a young imagination, knowing it would grow,
taking pleasure in the child's pleasure as it grew.

Writers themselves are working in the dark. We make our stories, and afterwards, sometimes we are lucky enough to see their
effect on other imaginations, and sometimes we haven't a clue
what happens. Nor do we know very much about the earlier links
in the chain: about the images and words that took root and
grew—and changed—in our own imaginations when we were
young. Sometimes those are so deep down, so long ago, that they
have been buried by time. Yet they work away unseen, ferment-
ing there in the dark unconscious, in ways that we may find out
only much later, and only by accident. I have a story to tell you
about that.

I still have some of the books that I loved when I was a child,
but not perhaps the most important ones. The only books I have
are those that retained their hard covers. Indeed two of them,
When We Were Very Young and *The House at Pooh Corner,* still
have their covers sheathed in the brown paper with which my
mother used to replace dust jackets as they fell off. But the very
best-loved books, of course, are so much handled that they are
likely to lose not just jackets but covers, and fall apart. Those I
no longer have.

When I was young, my mother, who was normally a most sensitive and thoughtful parent, did a terrible thing. She threw away

everything in my toy cupboard. I have to admit that I was twenty-two at the time. I hadn't actually played with any of the toys for some fifteen years, and I only spent the occasional weekend in the room which contained the toy cupboard, since I'd already been away at university for three years and was now living in an attic in Chelsea having a highly enjoyable adult life as a newspaper reporter. But what happened was that I came home one weekend and found that all my childhood companions had vanished, without my having been able to say good-bye to them. The toy cupboard wasn't completely empty, but it was dreadfully, unnaturally tidy. A few stuffed animals, and one doll, sat forlornly next to a half-shelf of books with covers—those are the survivors, the ones I still have. The major toys, a dollhouse, a farm and a wonderful garden, had been given to an orphanage, and everything else was gone. Just gone. Like my childhood, of course.

I didn't really mind the vanishing of the objects, though I mourn to this day one little lead soldier. Actually he was a sailor, a little blue walking figure in able seaman's uniform, whom I had always particularly loved even though his head was held on by a matchstick. (Or perhaps it was *because* his head was held on by a matchstick. You know how the English are.) But since I was already a writer, I mourned very greatly the loss of the ancient, tattered books, the fragments of books, which went right back to the days when I was first learning to read. These were the stories which had fed my burgeoning imagination, stories whose roots went so deep into my life that I could scarcely remember some of them at all. I felt obscurely that they were clues to some important creative mystery; that they should have been left in the cupboard, waiting, like fossils, until the day when I would excavate them and realize, with a cry of wonder, what they meant. But now they were gone. The mystery would never be solved, the meaning never found.

"They were falling apart," said my poor mother, in defense against my howls of anguish. "They were torn, and the pages were all mixed up, and they were full of moths and silverfish!"

And, she might have added but didn't, you grew up and moved out, and you always said you'd take your stuff out of that cupboard and you never did.

So down into oblivion went the secret map to my imagination, never to be recovered. I never forgot the loss, but gradually I forgot all the tantalizing echoes and shreds of memory of the books. They faded away. All except one. One book hovered at the back of my mind like a very distant, unintelligible little voice, calling. I could remember very little about this book; I didn't know who wrote it, I could barely recall what it was about. But I had a deep conviction that it was important. I went on living with this nagging little almost-memory for decades, never doing anything to seek it out because by now I lived in America, and I was pretty certain that the book in question was very English and certainly out of print.

Then one day in 1990, I gave a talk in Britain to some members of the Library Association, at a workshop held by their Young Libraries Group. I was listing the books that had most influenced me when I was very young, and in passing I mentioned this one, the unidentified ghost hovering at the edge of my memory. "I don't know its title or author," I told them. "All I can remember is that it took a sequence—perhaps alphabetical—of the more eccentric names of English villages (Upper Wittering, and things like that), and made up a highly unlikely story about the derivation of each. I adored it. If anyone remembers the name of this book, please tell me and I shall love you for life."

Nobody took up this generous offer. Nobody there knew what the book was. My talk was published in the Group's journal, the *Youth Library Review,* and none of its readers knew either. Or so I thought until 1991, when I had a letter from Romsey, in Hampshire, from a lady called Ruth Allen. She had been a librarian for twenty-two years and was now a bookseller, but she still took the journal of the Young Libraries Group and had just gotten around to reading her latest copy. Her letter said, "Someone may already have gained your love for life by identifying the

173

favorite book of your youth; however, not only do I think I know the book, but I also have a copy to sell! At the risk of losing the love to earn some money, here are its details."

And there was my ghost, identified in a catalogue listing:

> ELEANOR FARJEON, *Perkin the Pedlar*. Faber, 1st ed. 1932. Cloth covered bds in two shades of blue and white, eight full page coloured ills and numerous b&w ills by Claire Leighton. Edges a little rubbed. Pencilled inscription in childish hand on ffep.
>
> An alphabet of British place-names, with a story for each. £50.

"I am sorry if it seems expensive," said Ruth Allen, in her letter, but the book wouldn't have seemed expensive to me if it had cost £500. I sent her an ecstatic thank-you letter and a check and in due course *Perkin the Pedlar* arrived.

I opened the package very nervously. The book's cover showed a landscape of light blue hills and fields, edged with dark blue hedges, under a dark blue sky. A white road curved below the hills, toward a nestling village with a church spire. I didn't recognize it, because of course my hovering ghost-book had lost its cover, probably when I was about three. But when I opened the cover, the shock of recognition that came at me from the typeface, and the first of the strong line illustrations, was so powerful that I shut it again. I thought: *Reading this book is going to be special. I have to do it in the right place, and at the right time.*

After that, *Perkin the Pedlar* sat for almost two years on my bookshelf, a particular bookshelf near my bed where there's a hoard of unread books waiting to be discovered. I didn't forget it, I kept glancing to make sure it was there, but I wasn't in a hurry with this one; I was like a child saving up the last piece of chocolate. I only took the book down, in the end, when I began to think about the things I wanted to say at this institute. I felt, through some formless instinct, that it might be relevant. So I sat down one quiet day, turned off the telephone, and started to read.

There was once a place called Zeal Monachorum, and for the matter of that, there still is.

If you think it does not sound a very likely sort of place to be, for the matter of that, there once wasn't.

This is how it came to be.

One day a Wizard was walking along, and every here and there he came to a town or a village on his way. Presently he came to a big bare space, where there wasn't a place of any sort. So he stopped his walk, and stamped his foot, and turned around three times backwards, muttering,

"Zeal Monachorum!
High Cockalorum!
Above 'em,
Below 'em,
Behind 'em,
Before 'em!
Snip-Snap-Snorum!
Riddle-me-ree!
Zeal Monachorum—
So let it be!"

And so it was. A village sprang up, with a big sign in the middle saying ZEAL MONACHORUM, and the wizard nodded his head and went on with his walk. But there were no people in the village, until one day a man and his wife came along and decided to settle down there. They settled down with a vengeance, and they had twenty-six children, thirteen pairs of twins.

Each of the twenty-six children was named for a letter of the alphabet, from Anna to Zebediah. But although they were very bright children, who could recite the names of all the Kings and Queens of England, and their multiplication tables up to nine times nine, they *could* not say their ABC. "A is for strawberry," they would say when challenged. "B is for June." The only letter of the alphabet they really knew was Z, about which they would all shout with one voice, "Z is for Zeal Monachorum!"

175

Their sad lack of the Alphabet (said Eleanor Farjeon) bothered their parents greatly.

Then one day there was a knock at this family's door, and when the nearest child opened it, "there stood a queer little man in an old leather jacket and a ragged felt hat, stooping under a big bag slung across his back."

Now here I was, reading. And as I read those two lines, the hairs stood up on the back of my neck. Here and at half a dozen other points in this book, I was recognizing a magic—rediscovering certain very particular pictures that had lodged in my imagination fifty years before. The image of the queer little man, Perkin the wandering pedlar, was the first.

Then the story went on, and the hairs on the back of my neck lay down again. Perkin (said Eleanor Farjeon) was a pedlar of alphabets, and he made all his alphabets himself. There was an alphabet of trees, an alphabet of birds, and he had just finishing making an alphabet of places, and was rather footsore as a result. So he came to an agreement with the mother of the twenty-six bright but illiterate children: in exchange for a night's rest, and a good breakfast, he would teach all the twins their alphabet.

I read on.

Perkin the Pedlar said, "When I was walking Britain, looking for the first letter of my Alphabet, I came one day to a long, red wall with a green door in it. " And at this image the back of my neck prickled again, particularly when the door opened and he saw through it an endless orchard of apple trees, all bearing bright fruit, red and yellow and green. But although the story he then told was a pretty one, about the name of the town of Appledore, in the county of Kent, I didn't recognize it. The chord of music had come just for a moment—just from that wall, with the door in it, opening on to a different little world.

With the very next letter, the sense of recognition came back. Perkin the Pedlar came to a village where the air was thick with birds, driven by a great wind. He tried to pass through it from another direction, but there the wind blew sticks and stones and smoke at him—and on a third road, a hurricane of snowflakes was blowing a ship in full sail through the air. The fourth way was just as difficult, and Perkin called out to a girl being buffeted past him, "I want to get by!"

"They'll stop you if They can," said she.

(That's where the prickle of familiarity came—with that "They.")

"Who may They be?" said Perkin.

"The Blowers who live on the Green," she said—and he found himself in the middle of the village green, and there beside him were four figures, blowing for all they were worth.

One was a young man, and he blew south; one was an old man, and he blew east; one was in his prime, and he blew north, and one was a boy, and he blew west. The first blew through a flute, out of which a bird flew at every note; the second blew through a funnel, through which the smoke streamed out in clouds; the third blew through his fists, through which came sleet and hail, and the fourth blew through a clay pipe, from which came bubbles bright as sunshine and gay as wildflowers.

And when Perkin asked who they were, the boy said, in a pause for breath, "We are the Blowers, and we have to keep blowing night and day, so that the earth may be filled and the world may go round."

That was the story of a village called Blower's Green—they were all real places—in the county of Worcestershire, and now that I saw it again, it chimed in my memory, with its mysterious They and its sense of obligation, its mini-myth. I heard a strange faint echo again in the story of Chipping Norton, in Oxfordshire, where a stone breaker called Norton went on working and working, all day and every day, with never a pause for fun—and another echo in the story of Edenbridge, in Kent, where an ancient Adam and Eve dug and planted and pruned to make a wonderful garden that could never satisfy them, because it couldn't match the one they had lost.

"Don't you remember," said aged Eve, "how the bluebells spread like a lake under the young oak-trees? I'd like a lake of bluebells in our garden."

Then she said she wanted orange lilies, and red roses. And an apple tree.

"I'll do my best," said old Adam. "I'll try."

Poor Adam, doomed always to try, never to succeed. Or perhaps valiant Adam, who never stops trying, so long as he may live.

When Perkin reached the letter M, and the village of Much Wenlock, it was the modern middle-aged surface of my mind that reacted. He was in a town which once had been called Wenlock, then More Wenlock, then Much Wenlock—"and one of these days," said one of its inhabitants, "it will be Too Much Wenlock." And I thought, "Oh yes, I've seen a lot of that since the days when I first read this book, and so have we all—that's how we got Los Angeles."

But then Perkin the Pedlar hoisted a twin named Peter onto his knee and began telling the tale of a village in Gloucestershire whose name began with the letter P—and reading it, I was pulled so deep into memory that there was a prickling not at the back of my neck but in my eyes. Perkin was walking at night, and he heard a voice talking to itself, and small sounds, scritch-scratch, scritch-scratch. Pretty soon he came upon a little old man sitting in the middle of the road. (Eleanor Farjeon called this person a Gnome, and instantly I remembered that I had rejected that as twee when I was a child, and now I feel exactly the same and reject it still. Not a Gnome, Eleanor, please no. It doesn't fit.)

In the old man's hand

> there was a long thorn pierced at one end like a needle, and threaded with a strand of moonlight, and at his side he had a pile of scraps and pieces, which he was turning over busily to find the bit he wanted. Having found it, he laid it neatly over a hole or crack in the road to see if it fitted, and when he was satisfied, he began to stitch

it all round deftly with his needle of thorn and thread of the moon. The stitches made the scritch-scratch sound I had heard as I came up—said Perkin the Pedlar.

"Move out of my moonlight!" said the old man to him. "How can I do my work if you stand in my moonlight?"

"What is your work?" said Perkin.

"I patch the way—I mend the roads at night with anything that's been dropped there during the day. Birds' feathers, a child's penny, anything will do. . . . And new men will walk on the way made whole with what the last men lost there."

Then he stitched a crust of bread into a rather large hole,

and cocked his head this way and that at the square foot of the way he had covered with his patches—beside the crust [said Perkin] I could see a silver sixpence, a blue silk ribbon, the thumb of an old leather glove, and a bone button. The old man then took from his pouch a tiny wedge-shaped star, heated it at a glow-worm in the hedge, held it for a moment near his cheek to make sure it was not too hot, and with rapid movements slid his starry iron over the patches in the road. When he had done . . . the road was as white and smooth as though it was new-made.

The old man moved to another spot that needed patching. "Your shadow's in my way again," he said.

"Then I'll take myself off," said Perkin. "But before I go, I'd like to know what you call this spot."

"Patchway, stupid, Patchway," said the old man, and very deftly he patched the shadow of Perkin's pack into the road as he spoke.

"And never forget," said Perkin the Pedlar to the child on his knee, "that P is for Peter, and P is for Patchway, in the county of Gloucestershire."

Now as I read all that, it shone out of my lost and buried years like the old man's moonlight. This was one of the passages that had been lying there invisible, haunting me. I wasn't too sure about that glow-worm, I thought it might belong with the Gnome in tweeland, but criticism was not the name of this game. I was on a quest, though I wasn't quite sure for what. On I went through the pages, through the alphabet, waiting for my private Geiger counter to start crackling. For quite a while it was silent. I admired the ingenuity of the stories, as I read, but I found no other flicker of recognition—until I came to the letter S.

Here Perkin the Pedlar came to the sea, "a dark and rugged coast where the sea dashed itself among the rocks" like a giant millrace. He saw a seaman in a small boat heading to shore, tossing and lurching but at last managing to beach his boat.

"He came up to me," said Perkin, "wiping his wet face with the back of his hand."

"They all but had me that time," said he.

"Whom do you call They?" I asked.

"The Mills yonder—the grinding rocks and the wild water. Ah, Master Pedlar, every sailor on the sea knows he's grist for the Mills, if they can get him."

"What would happen then?" I asked.

"They'd grind him, Pedlar."

"What, into flour?"

"No, not flour. But something finer than he'd ever been in life. Look you there, now!"

I looked where his finger pointed to the seething waters [said Perkin] and tossed among them I saw a great company of people—men and women, boys and girls, sailors, soldiers, pirates, traders and judges, kings and stowaways, and even a poet. For one moment I saw them thus as they were when the Mills took them; then they vanished in the foam of the waters, and when next they appeared they were all changed; they rose up from the waters as light and white as foam, their bodies were fine and radiant, their hair was transparent, their eyes shining as stars; and up from the waves they floated like clouds in the morning, men and women, boys and girls, sailors, soldiers, pirates, traders and judges, kings and stowaways, with the poet leading them all. I watched them go, as bright as a flight of gulls, and as they vanished in the heavens I said to the man beside me,

"Why then, 'tis no bad thing to be ground in the Mills of the Sea."

"True enough," said he. . . .

"Has this place a name?" I asked.

"We call it Sea Mills," he said.

And so it was, a village in Eleanor Farjeon's favorite county of Gloucestershire. And the twin who sat on Perkin the Pedlar's knee as he told that story was called, I am happy to say, Susan. I hadn't remembered Susan, but I'd remembered, I certainly knew, the Mills of the Sea, and the people ground into air and light.

There was only one other place in the book that gave me the prickle of recognition, and it was no more than a moment: the faint strange sound of a bell ringing out of a wood, in the village of Yeavering Bell in Northumberland. "Almost the shadow of a sound, rather than the sound itself," Perkin said.

And when he had done with his alphabet and had Zebediah on his knee, the twenty-six children happily shouted aloud and in unison every letter and every town, in proper order, for the first time in their lives. And that was the end of the story.

I sat there with my rediscovered book on my lap, and looked out of the window and thought about those images that had lodged in my six-, seven-, eight-year-old imagination. The images that had lain there below the conscious surface, refusing to show themselves but still haunting me, making the book a persistent almost-memory that wouldn't go away.

Suddenly now I had these images again. It seemed to me that they were all images of the writer that I was going to become; of the "sub-creation," as Tolkien called it, that we are all privileged to practice if we are born with a talent for writing. Especially perhaps when we turn from reality to metaphor, and escape into fantasy. The long red wall with a green door in it, and a different

181

world beyond—every fantasy maker that ever was has used that door, in one way or another, from Spenser to C. S. Lewis. If Neanderthal Man had storytellers, there was probably one who said, in whatever grunts they used then, "Once upon a time there was a boy who went to the back of the cave and found a door, and he went through it, and on the other side he found . . ."

He found the lost world, perhaps, the one we all lose, the garden that Perkin the Pedlar's Adam and Eve were trying so longingly to remake. That was one of the images I remembered—now why did *that* stick in the mind of a child who had not yet learned about great loss? And why did the image of Norton, Chipping Norton, chipping away at his stone, working and working without a break? That's the way you work when you're writing a novel, when you may appear to pause for meals or sleep or bathing the children or going to the store but in fact you never pause at all, because your imagination is living not in the real world but in the one you are creating, in the task of sub-creation that goes on all the time, awake or asleep. Eleanor Farjeon knew about that, but I didn't, not then, not yet.

Instinctively I had picked up the images of making, and of mystery. The mysterious They: the Blowers blowing the world around, and the Mills of the Sea grinding people into light, into clouds of birds, into thin air. The sound of a bell ringing in a wood, beckoning, warning, announcing, celebrating. And the small nonhuman person sitting on a road in the moonlight, patching our way through this world with the fragments of ordinary life, and running his magic iron over them to make the way smooth for others to walk on. They are all metaphors of creativity. A metaphor, like any other aspect of poetry, is seldom created by the conscious mind; it tends to leap magically out of the imagination, which inhabits the unconscious mind. And when you read a metaphor, by the same token it's not your analytical mind but your imagination that like a hungry fish swallows the metaphor, chomp, without a beat. It moves, it's alive, gobble it up! So my very young imagination gobbled up all

182

these particular pictures which were metaphors, leaving behind all the rest, and drew them deep deep down inside, to haunt me for fifty years until the book from which they came drew them out again.

Holding the book, I thought: *That's extraordinary. That's wonderful.* But the book hadn't finished with me yet.

I looked down at the last page of *Perkin the Pedlar*, and I read it, and then I stared at it, and read it again—and I realized that I had never read it before. It had always been there, but I'd never noticed it. When I read the book this time, my attention had fallen away when Perkin completed his last alphabetical story— and so it must have done every time I read it as a child, because this last page rang no bells, prickled no skin, had never lodged in my imagination at all. Yet it was probably the most important page in the book.

The children happily recite their alphabet.

But before they could say Z (which they had known all along) Perkin the Pedlar jumped the last child off his knee, sprang to his feet, and cried,

"Never forget, my dears, that Z is for Zebediah, and Z is for—

"Zeal Monachorum!

High Cockalorum!

Above 'em,

Below 'em,

Behind 'em,

Before 'em!

Snip-Snap-Snorum!

Riddle-me-ree!

Zeal Monachorum—

So let it be!"

Then Perkin the Pedlar turned round three times backwards, stamped his foot, and vanished.

He was never seen in Zeal Monachorum again. And the children remembered their ABC for the rest of their lives.

And I thought: oh my Lord, *Perkin is the Wizard.* They're the same person. He isn't just a pedlar with a bag of alphabets; he's the all-powerful magician who made the place in the beginning. He cast the spell, and went on his way—and now he's done it again. That's something that my imagination didn't even notice, when I was a child.

But I could hardly fail to notice it now, because of course I've grown up to become Perkin the Pedlar, walking the world with my bag of words. Each one of us who works with words is Perkin, anyone who puts words on paper or reads them aloud. We tell stories to the children, stories that will hold them, entertain them, make them laugh or cry, and perhaps incidentally teach them something about living, about themselves, even about our language. Language is the foundation of Eleanor Farjeon's whole book: here is this wordmonger, with his bag full of names his audience has never heard before—and will now never forget.

And what about the structures that are built out of the words? *How do you think of your stories?*—that perennial question from the children. *Where do you get your ideas?*

Well—by magic. Magic is another word for mystery, and the creative process is a great mystery. So, Perkin is not only the wordmonger, he is the Wizard. He is Ged of Earthsea, he is Merriman, he is Ursula and Jill and John and Betty and Greg and Katherine and Sarah and all of us who write or draw. He brings places into being where none existed before, he can point a finger and bring to life a grown person whose characteristics even he doesn't yet fully know. By a particular magic—"this little miracle one performs," Ursula said—he can use everything he has ever seen or done or read, to make new stories, new images, new ideas. Oh yes, we work very hard to hone our craft, but we don't know *how* we connect with that shadowy part of the imagination out of which the words come—we just do it. We talk and talk about creativity, up and down and inside out, but we have never been able to define what it really is, and we never shall. It's a mystery, like time, and life, and death. Like the little green sprout that grows out of the hard dark seed.

All we can do, in the end, is celebrate the mystery. And make sure that we do everything possible to feed those young imaginations, in their joyous period of early discovery. You can't create creativity, but you can always nurture it, and cajole it, and challenge it to do its best.

I started with Wordsworth and I end with Christopher Logue: a small diamond of a poem that seems to me to say a lot about the imagination, about the young, and about the nature of an organization called Children's Literature New England.

> Come to the edge.
> We might fall.
> Come to the edge.
> It's too high!
>
> COME TO THE EDGE!
>
> And they came
> and he pushed
> and they flew . . .

AN INTERVIEW

Susan Cooper was interviewed in July 1989 by Professor Raymond Thompson of Acadia University, Nova Scotia.

What attracted you to the Arthurian legend as an ingredient in your series The Dark Is Rising?

I haven't the least idea. It never occurred to me that I was writing about Arthurian legend as such. I was just writing a series of fantasies which draw on everything I'd ever read, lived through, and absorbed through general cultural osmosis. The Matter of Britain was part of a great mass of stuff in my subconscious, which consisted of fairy tale, folktale, myth—that whole range of material that had always appealed to me enormously since childhood. I suppose I had read almost as much as was then in print, apart from very scholarly studies, about Arthurian legend, partly because I went to Oxford and the English School at Oxford is very strong on earlier literature.

So for you Arthurian legend was just one part of a wider tradition?

Yes. One result of coming to live in America in 1963 was that I became extremely homesick and turned to reading about not just England, but Britain. Perhaps if I had stayed in England I would have been less focused on things British. I have a strong sense of the mythic history of the land. I grew up in Buckinghamshire, in what was then a countryish area twenty-two miles outside London. I had an awareness of the past that I never had to think about. There was an Iron Age fort a couple of fields away. There was a Roman pavement that somebody had found in his field. Windsor Castle I could see from my bedroom window. Things like that give a sense of layers and layers of time, and of the stories that stick to those layers and develop through them, even though you may not realize that you've got it. It's a great legacy for a writer. I was lucky.

Did your appreciation of this legacy grow keener when you came to America?

I think so. The English author J. B. Priestley was a friend of mine, and he used to write to me when I was going through this dreadful homesick period. In one of his letters he said, do not worry about being away from your roots; you will find you write better about a place when you are away from it. That certainly turned out to be true with the *Dark Is Rising* books. They were immensely British, yet all except the first were written either here in Massachusetts, or on a very small island in the Caribbean where we have a house.

As a child, did you read Arthurian stories for younger readers?

I suppose I must have done because I knew the legends, but I couldn't tell you which ones specifically.

The experience at Oxford must have greatly increased your familiarity with Arthurian legend, then?

Yes. We had to do a lot of background reading in the French sources, such as Chretien de Troyes. I also read *The Mabinogion*, the chronicles, and many other works that I don't recall now. I didn't, however, refer back to the studies I did at Oxford when I wrote the books. No way. Whatever went into that room at the back of my head while I was at university, there it is in that room. I never consciously looked at it afterwards.

You didn't read Arthurian sources as a preparation for writing the books?

No. The only thing I ever reread on purpose is *The Mabinogion*, and that not very often. Malory I dip into just because I love the prose.

Did you read studies of the Arthurian era by archaeologists and historians?

Yes. I read Chambers and Loomis and Leslie Alcock, and I think John Morris's *Age of Arthur* is fascinating because of the different threads. They were part of my general reading, however, rather than preparation for the series. I'm the kind of person who would go into a secondhand bookshop and look around for anything in that area that I hadn't read.

Had you read any of the more modern versions of the Arthurian legend, such as Tennyson's Idylls of the King *and T. H. White's* The Once and Future King?

Oh sure. At university I probably read everything Tennyson ever wrote. T. H. White I loved, but I hadn't read many modern novels about Arthur before I wrote the series. It was only when I started *The Dark Is Rising*, the second book in the series, that I realized I had four more books to write. Once I found I was writing fantasy which was being published for young adults, I thought, it's very dangerous to read anybody who is writing in this area. So I didn't. As a result, when I finished the last book I had this lovely orgy reading Alan Garner, C. S. Lewis, and a whole bunch of other writers. I enjoyed them enormously, especially Alan Garner. He's wonderful. We met each other, he and I, at a conference years later. It was like meeting your brother!

Were you conscious of the fact that you were writing in the fantasy form in the Dark Is Rising *series, particularly the later books, since the fan-tasy element is less obvious in* Over Sea, Under Stone?

Evolution, that was, really. I wrote *Over Sea, Under Stone* when I was a very young journalist, before I left England. A publishing company called Jonathan Cape, which had published E. Nesbit, had a competition for a family adventure story, and I thought I would go in for this. So the book started off as an adventure story. It doesn't really draw much on Arthurian legend. It makes use of a grail, but not in the same way as the Grail legend. Very early on, however, this character called Merriman turned up, and the book turned itself into a fantasy. Once I was writing fantasy, I don't think I really thought about it. I just felt I'd come home. You don't say to yourself, I am writing fantasy. You don't even say to yourself, I am writing for kids. You just tell the story. Or you're really living in it and reporting on what you find. Of course what you find comes out of your own unconscious.

Did you have in mind a particular age group when you were writing the series?

No, I've never aimed at an age group. You write something and the publishers decide that. To some extent you're aware of your audience because you don't use enormously long Latinate words, for instance. Even then if somebody were to say, you can't use that word because it's too complicated, you can reply, let the kid look it up. This is the way children learn languages, by coming across words they haven't met before. I don't know who I'm writing for. I write for me, I suppose.

The conflict between good and evil, that is central to the series, is to some extent inherent in the Arthurian legend itself. Were you influenced by that when you were writing?

No. I take more from the chronicles and *The Mabinogion* than from the medieval romances where that conflict is more marked, though that is something I only recognize in retrospect. I'm more interested in Arthur as *dux bellorum*, as the Dark Ages war leader, than in the romantic image of the Round Table.

The struggle between the Light and the Dark in my books has more to do with the fact that when I was four World War II broke out. England was very nearly invaded by Germany, and that threat, reinforced by the experience of having people drop bombs on your head, led to a very strong sense of Us and Them. Of course Us is always good, and Them is always bad.

This sense must have stayed with me, and it put me into contact with all the other times that England has been threatened with invasion. We are such mongrels: we have been invaded over and over and over again from Scandinavia, from Ireland, from the Continent. This same fear and resistance—usually unsuccessful—has been repeated throughout British history. All that goes into the collective unconscious, and, especially if you come from a generation which went through this experience in childhood, it becomes very much a part of your own imagination. So there is this sympathetic link between my growing up and what it must have been like when the real Arthur—what we know about him—was alive. You find this reflected in the books, especially the last.

What is the relationship between Arthur and Herne the Hunter in your series?

One of the things I tend to believe, largely as a result of reading Robert Graves, whom I'm sure many scholars find outrageous, is that there is a blurring of identity between an awful lot of figures. The mythic territory of the totally mythical Herne and the possibly-once-real Arthur can cross and overlap, and this happens with the figures in my story. So it is never possible to say, this character is precisely this, and that one is precisely that, because nothing is precise in myth. When you're using myth you can be precise for the purposes of your book, but you do it at your own peril. The mythic elements are all intended to be slightly out of focus, like an impressionist painting, and if you try to sharpen the focus you will lose something. You will lose the magic. The writer must tread gently.

During the last battle in the final book, Arthur seems to disappear. Why was that?

I don't know. That's just the way it happened. This is the story of the Dark and the Light, not a story about Arthur. It draws on myth only to the extent that the myth serves the story. The major Arthurian figure in my series is one that doesn't exist in Arthurian legend: Bran, the son of Arthur. He is my invention. It's with great temerity that an author departs from tradition like this, but you just do it. I think perhaps that he originates in the very strong image of betrayal that you find in the story of Arthur, Guinevere and Lancelot.

Why did you decide to make Bran the son of Arthur, rather than just an ordinary figure?

I don't know. It was not a rational decision. I start a book knowing it's a road. You know the beginning, you know who's going with you on the road, you know roughly where they're going, but you don't know anything at all (at least I don't) about what's going to happen on the way. You find out as you go along. When I write a novel, I have two things. I have the manuscript as it comes out very slowly, from the typewriter or on the page or wherever; and at the same time I keep a notebook.

It's full of random scraps from all over the place, and they often turn up in the books: quotations, images, historical allusions, et cetera. But in it I also talk to myself. I'm sure if I looked back at the notebook for *The Grey King*, I would find at some point a realization that Bran is going to be the son of Arthur, just as there was a point at which Merriman turned out to be Merlin. Your head does things before it tells you it's doing them.

At what point did you recognize that Merriman was Merlin?

At the end of *Over Sea, Under Stone* one of the characters, a small boy called Barney, says, "Merry Lyon . . . Merlion . . . *Merlin*" (218). It was only when I reached that point in the writing that I realized who he was. I recognized it at the same time as Barney did. There must be some Jungian reason why the Merlin figure has a particular attraction for me, but I've never delved into it.

Once you discovered Merriman Lyon was Merlin, did that place restraints upon how you were able to use him as a character because of the way he appears in tradition?

No, he's my character. He's not the Merlin of tradition. Merriman is an Old One in my books, a figure of the Light that opposes the Dark, which is my rather obvious classification of good and evil. He doesn't have the ambiguous dark qualities of Merlin in Arthurian legend. The sinister side of Merriman Lyon, and indeed all the Old Ones, is that absolute good, like absolute evil, is fanatical. As one of my characters points out, there is no room for human ambiguity. Absolute good is like a blinding light, which can be very cruel, and to that extent Merriman is not a sympathetic character. He represents something, but what he represents is to do with those books and not to do with Arthurian legend.

Were you aware that Taliesin had Arthurian associations when you included him in Silver on the Tree, *the concluding novel in the series?*

No, I probably wasn't. I think he may have come from Robert Graves's *The White Goddess,* which I read while writing the series.

Do you have specific locations in mind for your settings, or are they an amalgamation?

Oh, very specific. *Over Sea, Under Stone* and *Greenwitch* are both set in Trewissick, which is based on a village in southern Cornwall called Mevagissey. We used to go there when I was a child. *The Dark Is Rising* is set in the part of Buckinghamshire where I grew up. Every stick is real. It doesn't look that way now, a lot of it, but some of it does. The little church is still exactly the same. Huntercombe is based upon the village of Dorney and the Great Hall is Dorney Court, which I see is being used as Miss Haversham's house in a new television version of Dickens's *Great Expectations.* The Welsh setting in *The Grey King* and *Silver on the Tree* is around Aberdyfi, the village where my grandmother was born and where my parents lived. I took some liberties with the description at one point, combining two valleys into one, but otherwise it's exact. My aunt who still lives there occasionally has people knocking on the door and saying, is this the certain point from that book?

Did you need to check details of the topography after you had started writing, or was your recollection clear enough?

I had two ordnance survey maps pinned up in my study inside a cupboard door, so that if I wanted to check them I went to the cupboard. Also I used to go home every year. I can remember going out of the door from my parents' house when I was visiting Aberdyfi from America, to remind myself what it was like to go across the dunes and down to the sea in the very early morning.

The images that I encountered on the way went into *Silver on the Tree,* where a character called Jane does just that. So I did things like that.

An awful lot of detail comes out of your memory, however. You don't know it's there until you start writing about it. In that same book Will and Bran are on a mountaintop on one side of the River Dyfi, and there appears a magical arching bridge which takes them down into a timeless place called the Lost Land. When I was writing that passage I had them on the mountaintop, and I didn't know what happened next. Then I remembered, the last time I was home—being up on that particular mountain, looking out across the estuary of the River Dyfi. Ever since I was a child I had known the legend about the drowned country, and I could almost see it. As I recalled that moment I thought, that's what they do! That's what happens. That's what I meant by saying it's not a rational decision. You can't control it. You say, oh, I *see!* You even find yourself using images from dreams sometimes.

Were you aware of legends about Arthur attached to any of these places?

Yes. In the valley behind Aberdyfi, for example, is a stone where King Arthur's horse is supposed to have left a hoofprint. I'm interested in the creation of layers of myth. You can really see how the Arthurian legend has developed, and why it is so impossible to go backwards and say, this bit is true and this isn't. It's all true. How much of it is real is another matter—and really irrelevant. This is like Camelot. Where was Camelot? Who cares really? It doesn't matter.

The books comprise a series. Did you find that what you had written in the earlier books committed you to directions that you subsequently regretted, or wished you had more freedom to change?

No. It was wonderful. It was like writing a symphony, in which each movement is different and yet they all link together. I wish

194

my imagination would give me another shape like that because there are all kinds of satisfactions inside it. Things link together, an early book leads to something in a later book. When I wrote the first book, of course, I didn't envision a series, but later, when I first had the idea of writing, not just the second book, but the whole sequence, I drew up a plan on a piece of paper. I had little notes written down: I had the four times of the year—focused upon the solstices, Beltane, and such festivals—I had places, and, very roughly, the characters who were in each book. I remember that under *The Grey King* there was a boy called Bran, but I didn't know who he was. So that was the only thing that limited me.

There were things I had to remember from early books that had to be either resolved or referred to in later books. Once in a great while some particularly bright child will write me a letter saying, you never said what happened to . . . But I didn't find it restricting. No.

Are there any particular details you would like to change, looking back in retrospect?

I would like to have developed the three Drew children more fully in the first book. They develop as the series progresses, but they're very corny kids' book characters in *Over Sea, Under Stone*, it seems to me. I hadn't gotten to know them.

As the series progresses, Jane in particular grows more interesting, doesn't she?

Yes. Jane is someone I always wanted to write about again. *Silver on the Tree* suffered from being the last book where I was tying up all the ends. It had too much in it. My head was going off in all directions. Its structure is not terrific. There was even more in it, but I took some of it out. Of course when you're dealing with the substance of myth, which is the fight between good and evil, I suppose, you have to provide the ultimate, terrific, enormous climax. It's almost impossible.

Did the elements you had drawn from Arthurian legend contribute significantly to that feeling of congestion?

I had to move away from it because it seems to me that the Arthurian legend is parallel to the Christian story of the leader who dies for salvation. Whereas what my books were trying to say is that nobody else can save us. We have to save ourselves. *Silver on the Tree* contains a reference to a poem that I remember my mother reciting to me. It's about Drake being in his hammock, which recalls the local legend in Devon that Sir Francis Drake will come back to rescue England if we're ever invaded again. Similarly, Arthur will come back, and Christ—they are saviors. I didn't want to use that idea. The Arthur that I was using goes to Avalon, but saving the world is up to the people in it.

So in a sense you had to keep Arthur from taking too strong a role within the story, didn't you?

Yes. It wasn't a case of Arthur coming into the story, however, rather a case of the story moving into the time of Arthurian legend, because that is what happens. These books go in and out of time, traveling like a train or a boat, linking one part to another to form a continuity.

I recognize that Arthurian legend is but one among many elements in your story, but what part of that legend did you feel was most important for you to include for your purposes?

I didn't go to the legend. The legend is there at the back of the imagination, in that room where the imagination goes sometimes to draw on something. The part of you that's writing the story at a certain point reaches out and says, I want that bit. You don't sit down at the desk saying, today I'm going to use that bit. It's as if you're going into a garden to pick something that you're going to cook for dinner. You don't say, today I want carrots and onions and green peppers. You go in and say to yourself, the broccoli looks good; I'll have some of that; there is one pepper on that bush; I'll take that. It's not organized. It's also as if something comes to help. Elements seem to say, I am here and I belong in this part of the story.

Of course picking, itself, is not the best image either, because the act of picking something is deliberate. It is very much a case of your consciousness being invaded at a certain point by something which belongs there.

What you get then is Merriman, who's a guide for young people?

Or Jung's wise old man.

And Arthur, who sides with the Light in the struggle against the Dark?

Yes. He represents the Light, I suppose.

They appear in the series because they emerge from your creative subconscious?

We are all writing about the same things in the end. Nobody ever invents a totally original character or story. You're lucky if you can be part of the fabric.

Have you any final comments?

I should just repeat that I've never sat down and thought about the way I've "used" the Arthurian legend, or the Matter of Britain as I like to call it, why certain parts of it come into the story and not other parts. The imagination makes its own choices.

PERMISSIONS FOR *Dreams and Wishes*

Acknowledgments to the literary trustees of Walter de la Mare, and the Society of Authors as their representative, for extracts from Walter de la Mare's anthology *Come Hither*; to Professor Raymond Thompson of Acadia University, Nova Scotia, for the interview with Susan Cooper; to Christopher Logue for his poem "Come to the Edge"; and to Ursula Le Guin for quotations from her book *Very Far Away from Anywhere Else.*

"Seeing Around Corners," "Fantasy in the Real World," and "Nahum Tarune's Book" were first published in *The Horn Book Magazine.*